用英語演講，培養自信

　　大多數人都同意，學英文應該從兒童時期開始，但是，小朋友缺乏耐心，東學一點、西學一點，模模糊糊，自己也搞不清楚學了什麼，今天學的，明天就忘記了。再加上要學會話、學文法、學 KK 音標、還要背單字，許多人反而因此對英文產生恐懼，對他們未來的學習造成負面的影響。

向長時間英語演講挑戰

　　其實，小朋友的學習能力很強、記憶力又好，背東西的速度非常快，只要有正確的方法和教材，一定可以發揮極大的學習效率。「一口氣兒童英語演講」專門為兒童設計，每一篇演講稿有 27 句，以三句為一組，九句為一段，共三段，孩子背起來沒有壓力。一般的演講稿背多了，背了後面就忘了前面。「一口氣兒童英語演講」是固定格式，可以一篇接一篇地背，小朋友會越背越想背，而且越背越快、越熟練，不斷地向長時間英語演講挑戰。

　　書中的每篇演講稿，正常速度是一分半鐘講完，如果能背到 50 秒鐘之內，就能變成直覺，終生不會忘記。演講稿的內容取材自美國人日常生活會話，平易近人，只要背熟，都可以運用在實際生活當中。由於孩子們所背的每一句英文，都是正確的、優美的句子，所以，他們不管是演講或說話時，都會很有信心。

用英語演講是說英文的最高境界，背演講是學英文最好的方法。「一口氣兒童英語演講」的發明，是「學習出版公司」最新研發的成果，也是目前所有兒童英語教材中，獨一無二的產品。在本書出版之前，這套教材已經在幾所著名小學實際使用過，效果卓著。大部分小朋友都很有表演欲，在學校裡學了什麼，回家就會秀給爸爸媽媽看，這是很棒的親子互動。同樣地，孩子們背了英語演講，回到家，每次全家吃飯前，都可以表演給大家看，必定能夠增加他們的氣質和自信心。

背演講需要有聽眾

背演講最簡單的方法，就是要有聽眾。孩子在家裡，背給所有家人聽，一背再背，熟能生巧。小孩子舌頭靈活，只要背了幾篇演講後，說起話來就字正腔圓，發音就像美國人一樣了，不必擔心會有口音的問題。現在我們只要花一點功夫來協助他們，對他們的未來就會大有幫助。孩子們現在的一小步，就等於他們未來的一大步。

小孩子剛開始背演講時，也許速度會很慢，但是會漸入佳境。背了幾篇演講稿之後，也可換換口味，改背「一口氣英語」。如此一來，小朋友不但會說流利的英文，更能用英文發表演講，英文實力自然領先別人。只要讓孩子養成自言自語說英文的習慣，英文很快就會變成他自己的語言。

劉毅

CONTENTS

1. Self-introduction

1

Ladies and gentlemen:
I'm happy to be here.
I'd like to introduce myself.

My name is Pat.
Everyone calls me Pat.
You can call me Pat.

I'm from Taiwan.
I was born in Taiwan.
I grew up in Taiwan.

introduction〔ˌɪntrə'dʌkʃən〕
self-introduction   lady〔'ledɪ〕
gentleman〔'dʒɛntḷmən〕   *I'd like to*
introduce〔ˌɪntrə'djus〕   myself〔maɪ'sɛlf〕
call〔kɔl〕   Taiwan〔'taɪ'wɑn〕
bear〔bɛr〕   *be born*
grow up

1

***Right now*, *I'm a student*.**

I'm eager to learn.

I study very hard every day.

I like being a student.

I like going to school.

I think it's interesting and fun.

I'm also learning English.

I enjoy speaking English.

It's my favorite class.

right now	eager〔'igɚ〕
study〔'stʌdɪ〕	hard〔hɑrd〕
interesting〔'ɪntrɪstɪŋ〕	
fun〔fʌn〕	learn〔lɜn〕
enjoy〔ɪn'dʒɔɪ〕	speak〔spik〕
favorite〔'fevərɪt〕	

1

***I*'m a friendly person.**

I always try to be polite.

I like to get along with everyone.

I want to be your friend.

I hope we can meet.

What do you say?

Let's be friends.

Let's get together.

Please introduce yourself.

---

friendly ('frɛndlɪ)   person ('pɝsn̩)

try (traɪ)   polite (pə'laɪt)

get along   want (wɑnt)

friend (frɛnd)   hope (hop)

meet (mit)   together (tə'gɛðɚ)

get together   yourself (jʊr'sɛlf)

1

 # 1.Self-introduction

🔵 演講解說

Ladies and gentlemen:	各位先生，各位女士：
I'm happy to be here.	很高興來到這裡。
I'd like to introduce myself.	我想要介紹我自己。
My name is Pat.	我的名字是派特。
Everyone calls me Pat.	每個人都叫我派特。
You can call me Pat.	你們可以叫我派特。
I'm from Taiwan.	我來自台灣。
I was born in Taiwan.	我在台灣出生。
I grew up in Taiwan.	我在台灣長大。

✳✳ ─────────────────────

introduction〔͵ɪntrə'dʌkʃən〕*n.* 介紹
self-introduction 自我介紹　　lady〔'ledɪ〕*n.* 女士；小姐
gentleman〔'dʒɛntḷmən〕*n.* 先生；男士
I'd like to 我想要 (= *I would like to*)
introduce〔͵ɪntrə'djus〕*v.* 介紹　　myself〔maɪ'sɛlf〕*pron.* 我自己
call〔kɔl〕*v.* 稱呼；叫　　Taiwan〔'taɪ'wɑn〕*n.* 台灣
bear〔bɛr〕*v.* 生　　***be born*** 出生　　***grow up*** 長大

***Right now*, *I'm a student*.**	現在，我是個學生。
I'm eager to learn.	我渴望學習。
I study very hard every day.	我每天都很努力唸書。
I like being a student.	我喜歡當學生。
I like going to school.	我喜歡去上學。
I think it's interesting and fun.	我認為那非常有趣。
I'm also learning English.	我也在學英文。
I enjoy speaking English.	我喜歡說英文。
It's my favorite class.	那是我最喜歡的課。

1

** ─────────────────

right now 現在（是 now 的加強語氣）

eager〔'igɚ〕*adj.* 渴望的　　study〔'stʌdɪ〕*v.* 學習；研讀

hard〔hɑrd〕*adv.* 努力地

interesting〔'ɪntrɪstɪŋ〕*adj.* 有趣的

fun〔fʌn〕*adj.* 有趣的　　learn〔lɝn〕*v.* 學習

enjoy〔ɪn'dʒɔɪ〕*v.* 喜歡　　speak〔spik〕*v.* 說

favorite〔'fevərɪt〕*adj.* 最喜歡的

1

I'm a friendly person.　　　　　　我是個親切的人。

I always try to be polite.　　　　　我總是試著要有禮貌。

I like to get along with　　　　　　我喜歡和大家好好相處。
　　everyone.

I want to be your friend.　　　　　我想做你們的朋友。

I hope we can meet.　　　　　　　我希望能認識你們。

What do you say?　　　　　　　　　你們說好不好？

Let's be friends.　　　　　　　　　我們來當朋友吧。

Let's get together.　　　　　　　　讓我們聚在一起。

Please introduce yourself.　　　　　請你們介紹一下自己。

＊＊ ─────────────────────

friendly〔'frɛndlɪ〕*adj.* 友善的；親切的

person〔'pɝsṇ〕*n.* 人　　　try〔traɪ〕*v.* 試著

polite〔pə'laɪt〕*adj.* 有禮貌的　　　***get along*** 相處；處得好

want〔wɑnt〕*v.* 想要　　　friend〔frɛnd〕*n.* 朋友

hope〔hop〕*v.* 希望　　　meet〔mit〕*v.* 認識

together〔tə'gɛðɚ〕*adv.* 一起　　　***get together*** 聚在一起

yourself〔jʊr'sɛlf〕*pron.* 你自己

●背景說明

　　我們每到一個新環境，都要先自我介紹。爲什麼要自我介紹呢？因爲這是讓別人認識你最快的方式。把你的名字、興趣和個性告訴大家，那麼很快地，你就會和每個人都成爲朋友。

1. ***I'd like to introduce myself.***

I'd like to 我想要（= *I would like to* = *I want to*）
introduce〔͵ɪntrəˋdjus〕*v.* 介紹
myself〔maɪˋsɛlf〕*pron.* 我自己

　　　　I'd like to 等於 I would like to，意思是「我想要」（= *I want to*），不要和 I like（我喜歡）混淆。

　　　　I'd like to introduce myself. 的意思是「我想要介紹我自己。」美國人也常說成：Let me introduce myself.（讓我來介紹我自己。）或 Allow me to introduce myself.（讓我來介紹我自己。）
【let〔lɛt〕*v.* 讓　　allow〔əˋlaʊ〕*v.* 允許】

【比較】下面三句意義相同：

　　　***I'd like to introduce myself.*【第一常用】**
　　　= I would like to introduce myself.【第二常用】
　　　= I want to introduce myself.【第三常用】

1

2. *My name is Pat.*
   Everyone calls me Pat.
   You can call me Pat.

Pat〔pæt〕*n.* 派特　　call〔kɔl〕*v.* 稱呼；叫

　　　Pat（派特）是男女都可以用的名字，這個名字不錯，如果你沒有英文名字的話，你就可以用。

　　　Pat 是名字，如果你姓「劉」，你的英文全名就是 Pat Liu。

　　　如果你要把名字告訴大家，有很多種說法：

(1) 介紹自己的名字（按使用頻率排列）：

　① *My name is Pat.*【第一常用】
　　（我的名字是派特。）

　② I'm Pat.（我是派特。）【第二常用】

　③ My English name is Pat.【第三常用】
　　（我的英文名字是派特。）

　④ My first name is Pat.（我的名字是派特。）
　　【*first name* 名字（last name 則是「姓」）】

(2) 告訴大家怎麼稱呼你（按使用頻率排列）：

　① *You can call me Pat.*【第一常用】
　　（你可以叫我派特。）

　② Please call me Pat.（請叫我派特。）【第二常用】

　③ Just call me Pat.（叫我派特就好。）【第三常用】

④ ***Everyone calls me Pat.*** （大家都叫我派特。）

⑤ All my friends call me Pat.
（我的朋友都叫我派特。）

⑥ Most people call me Pat.
（大多數的人都叫我派特。）

⑦ Feel free to call me Pat. （叫我派特沒關係。）

【most〔most〕*adj.* 大多數的　***feel free to V.*** 請自由地～】

3. *I'm from Taiwan.*
I was born in Taiwan.
I grew up in Taiwan.

Taiwan〔'taɪ'wɑn〕*n.* 台灣
bear〔bɛr〕*v.* 生　***be born*** 出生
grow up 長大

這三句話的意思是「我來自台灣。我在台灣出生。我在台灣長大。」

當你要介紹自己是哪裡人時，在英文裡有非常多種說法，我們依照使用頻率排列如下：

① ***I'm from Taiwan.***【第一常用】
（我來自台灣；我是台灣人。）

② I come from Taiwan. （我來自台灣。）【第二常用】

③ ***I was born in Taiwan.***【第三常用】
（我在台灣出生。）

④ I'm a native of Taiwan. （我是台灣人。）

【***come from*** 來自　native〔'netɪv〕*n.* 本地人】

1

4. *I enjoy speaking English.*

enjoy〔ɪnˈdʒɔɪ〕*v.* 喜歡   speak〔spik〕*v.* 說

這句話的意思是「我喜歡說英文。」enjoy 這個字常作「享受」解，但在這裡是「喜歡」的意思，就等於 like。但是要特別注意的是，enjoy 後面只能接動名詞 (V-ing)，但是 like 可接不定詞 (to V.) 或動名詞：

【比較】 *I enjoy speaking English.*【正】
　　　　 I enjoy to speak English.【誤】

另外，當你說自己「喜歡」某個人的時候，只能用 like，不能用 enjoy，你只要記住 enjoy 有「享受」的意思，而你不可能享受人，所以喜歡某個人，要用 like。

【比較】 *I like Michael Jordan.*【正】
　　　　 （我喜歡麥可喬登。）
　　　　 I enjoy Michael Jordan.【誤】

5. *I'm a friendly person.*

friendly〔ˈfrɛndlɪ〕*adj.* 友善的；親切的

這句話的意思是「我是個親切的人。」在自我介紹時，可以多用一些好的形容詞來形容自己，例如：humorous (幽默的)、polite (有禮貌的)、generous (慷慨的)、honest (誠實的)、tender (溫柔的) 等。

humorous〔ˈhjumərəs〕*adj.* 幽默的
polite〔pəˈlaɪt〕*adj.* 有禮貌的
generous〔ˈdʒɛnərəs〕*adj.* 慷慨的
honest〔ˈɑnɪst〕*adj.* 誠實的   tender〔ˈtɛndɚ〕*adj.* 溫柔的

6. *I like to get along with everyone.*
   get along 相處；處得好

這句話的意思是「我喜歡和大家好好相處。」也可以說成：I like to be friends with everybody. (我喜歡和大家做朋友。) ***get along*** 是作「相處；處得好」解，其用法舉例如下：

How do you ***get along*** with your brother?
(你和你哥處得怎麼樣？)
Cats and birds usually don't ***get along***.
(貓和鳥通常都合不來。)
【usually 〔ˈjuʒʊəlɪ〕*adv.* 通常】

7. *What do you say?*

這句話的意思是「你們說好不好？」在你自我介紹時，如果想要和台下的人多一點互動，你可以說這句話，如果聽眾們微笑，就表示他們已經開始對你有好感了。

這句話還有其他的說法，我們依照使用頻率排列如下：

① ***What do you say?*** (你們說好不好？)【第一常用】
② What do you think?【第二常用】
(你們覺得如何？)
③ How does that sound?【第三常用】
(你們覺得聽起來如何？)【sound 〔saʊnd〕*v.* 聽起來】
④ How do you feel about that?
(你們覺得怎麼樣？)

● 作文範例

Self-introduction

Introducing yourself is very important when you meet new people. You always want to make a good impression when telling others about yourself. Allow me to introduce myself.

My name is Pat and I'm from Taiwan. Right now, I'm a student. I study very hard every day. I like going to school because I'm eager to learn. I enjoy learning English. It's my favorite class. I like to make friends and I get along with everyone. This is the introduction I give whenever I meet new people. It tells people a little bit about me and about what I like to do.

● 中文翻譯

自 我 介 紹

當你認識新的人時，介紹自己是非常重要的。你一定會想要在告訴別人有關自己的事時，給別人留下好印象。讓我來介紹我自己。

我的名字是派特，我來自台灣。我現在是學生。我每天都很用功唸書。我喜歡上學，因為我渴望學習。我喜歡學英文。那是我最喜歡的課程。我喜歡交朋友，而且我和每個人都處得很好。這就是我每次認識新的人時，所做的自我介紹。它可以告訴別人一點關於我的事，還有我喜歡做什麼。

2. My Hobbies

2

I have many hobbies.
I like to do many things.
Let me share a few.

I like video games.
Computer games are cool, too.
I could play them all day.

I like collecting cards.
I play games with them.
I trade them with my friends.

hobby〔'hɑbɪ〕
share〔ʃɛr〕
video〔'vɪdɪ,o〕
computer〔kəm'pjutɚ〕
collect〔kə'lɛkt〕
trade〔tred〕
friend〔frɛnd〕

let〔lɛt〕
a few
video games
cool〔kul〕
card〔kɑrd〕

2

***Also*, *I like sports*.**

I like being outdoors.

I love fresh air and sunshine.

Bike riding is fun.

Rollerblading is neat.

Swimming is my favorite.

In addition, I like to draw pictures.

I like to read comics.

But please don't tell my parents.

---

also ('ɔlso)

be (bi)

love (lʌv)

air (ɛr)

bike (baɪk)

fun (fʌn)

neat (nit)

favorite ('fevərɪt)

draw (drɔ)

read (rid)

tell (tɛl)

sport (sport)

outdoors ('aʊt'dorz)

fresh (frɛʃ)

sunshine ('sʌn,ʃaɪn)

ride (raɪd)

rollerblade ('rolɚ,bled)

swim (swɪm)

in addition

picture ('pɪktʃɚ)

comic ('kɑmɪk)

parents ('pɛrənts)

Furthermore, *I like music*.

I like to sing songs.

I'm learning to play an instrument.

Of course, I enjoy learning English.

I like speaking with foreigners.

I love watching Disney cartoons.

There is more I like to do.

There is more I can say.

I'll save it for another day.

---

furthermore (ˈfɝðɚˌmor)

music (ˈmjuzɪk)   sing (sɪŋ)

song (sɔŋ)   learn (lɝn)

instrument (ˈɪnstrəmənt)

of course   enjoy (ɪnˈdʒɔɪ)

speak (spik)   foreigner (ˈfɔrɪnɚ)

watch (watʃ)   Disney (ˈdɪznɪ)

cartoon (karˈtun)   say (se)

save (sev)   another (əˈnʌðɚ)

2. My Hobbies

2

I have many hobbies.	我有很多嗜好。
I like to do many things.	我喜歡做的事很多。
Let me share a few.	讓我來告訴你們一些。
I like video games.	我喜歡電動玩具。
Computer games are cool, too.	電腦遊戲也很棒。
I could play them all day.	我可以玩這些東西一整天。
I like collecting cards.	我喜歡收集卡片。
I play games with them.	我用它們來玩遊戲。
I trade them with my friends.	我會和朋友交換卡片。

＊＊ ——————————————

hobby〔'hɑbɪ〕*n.* 嗜好　　let〔lɛt〕*v.* 讓
share〔ʃɛr〕*v.* 分享；告訴　　*a few* 一些
video〔'vɪdɪ,o〕*adj.* 電視的　　*video games* 電動玩具
computer〔kəm'pjutɚ〕*n.* 電腦　　cool〔kul〕*adj.* 很棒的
could〔kʊd〕*aux.* 可以　　*all day* 一整天
collect〔kə'lɛkt〕*v.* 收集　　card〔kɑrd〕*n.* 卡片
trade〔tred〕*v.* 交換　　friend〔frɛnd〕*n.* 朋友

2

Also, *I like sports*.　　　　　　　　我還喜歡運動。

I like being outdoors.　　　　　　　我喜歡待在戶外。

I love fresh air and sunshine.　　　我喜歡新鮮的空氣和陽光。

Bike riding is fun.　　　　　　　　　騎腳踏車很有趣。

Rollerblading is neat.　　　　　　　　溜直排輪很棒。

Swimming is my favorite.　　　　　　游泳是我最喜歡的運動。

In addition, I like to draw　　　　　另外，我喜歡畫圖。
　　pictures.

I like to read comics.　　　　　　　我喜歡看漫畫書。

But please don't tell my parents.　　但是請不要告訴我爸媽。

** ────────────────

also〔'ɔlso〕*adv.* 還　　sport〔sport〕*n.* 運動

be〔bi〕*v.* 在；位於　　outdoors〔'aut'dorz〕*adv.* 在戶外

love〔lʌv〕*v.* 喜歡　　fresh〔frɛʃ〕*adj.* 新鮮的

air〔ɛr〕*n.* 空氣　　sunshine〔'sʌnˌʃaɪn〕*n.* 陽光

bike〔baɪk〕*n.* 腳踏車　　riding〔'raɪdɪŋ〕*n.* 乘騎

fun〔fʌn〕*adj.* 有趣的　　rollerblading〔'rolɚˌbledɪŋ〕*n.* 溜直排輪

neat〔nit〕*adj.* 很棒的　　swimming〔'swɪmɪŋ〕*n.* 游泳

favorite〔'fevərɪt〕*adj.* 最喜歡的　　*in addition* 另外

draw〔drɔ〕*v.* 畫　　picture〔'pɪktʃɚ〕*n.* 圖畫

read〔rid〕*v.* 閱讀　　comic〔'kɑmɪk〕*n.* 漫畫書

please〔pliz〕*adv.* 請　　tell〔tɛl〕*v.* 告訴

parents〔'pɛrənts〕*n.pl.* 父母

2

Furthermore, ***I like music***.　　　　而且，我喜歡音樂。

I like to sing songs.　　　　　　我喜歡唱歌。

I'm learning to play an　　　　　我正在學習演奏樂器。
instrument.

Of course, I enjoy learning　　　當然，我也喜歡學英文。
English.

I like speaking with foreigners.　我喜歡和外國人說話。

I love watching Disney　　　　　我愛看迪士尼卡通。
cartoons.

There is more I like to do.　　　我喜歡做的事還有很多。

There is more I can say.　　　　我還可以說更多。

I'll save it for another day.　　　我會把它留到改天再說。

** ──────────────

furthermore〔ˋfɝðɚˌmor〕 *adv.* 此外；而且

music〔ˋmjuzɪk〕 *n.* 音樂　　sing〔sɪŋ〕 *v.* 唱

song〔sɔŋ〕 *n.* 歌曲　　learn〔lɝn〕 *v.* 學習

play〔ple〕 *v.* 演奏　　instrument〔ˋɪnstrəmənt〕 *n.* 樂器

of course 當然　　enjoy〔ɪnˋdʒɔɪ〕 *v.* 喜歡

speak〔spik〕 *v.* 說話　　foreigner〔ˋfɔrɪnɚ〕 *n.* 外國人

watch〔wɑtʃ〕 *v.* 看　　Disney〔ˋdɪznɪ〕 *n.* 迪士尼

cartoon〔kɑrˋtun〕 *n.* 卡通　　say〔se〕 *v.* 說

save〔sev〕 *v.* 保留　　another〔əˋnʌðɚ〕 *adj.* 另一的

◎ 背景說明

　　培養良好的嗜好，可以讓生活更加多采多姿。有些人的嗜好是運動，有些人則是喜歡背「一口氣英語」。本篇演講稿要教你用英文來介紹自己的嗜好，把你的嗜好告訴大家，有助於你找到志趣相投的朋友。

1. *Let me share a few.*

　　let〔lɛt〕v. 讓　　share〔ʃɛr〕v. 分享；告訴　　*a few* 一些

　　這句話的意思是「讓我來告訴你們一些。」*a few* 這個片語一般是當形容詞用，作「一些」解，用來形容可數名詞，例如：He has *a few* friends.（他有一些朋友。）但在這裡，a few 後面沒有接名詞，所以它是當代名詞用，代替複數名詞，作「一些；幾個」解。例如：

Only *a few* were chosen.（只有幾個人被選中。）
The teacher asked *a few* to recite.
（老師要求一些學生背書。）

【choose〔tʃuz〕v. 選擇　　recite〔rɪ'saɪt〕v. 背誦】

　　另外，share 的主要意思是「分享」，但在這裡，是引申作「告訴」解。例如：The history teacher *shared* many interesting stories with us.（歷史老師告訴我們很多有趣的歷史故事。）

history〔'hɪstrɪ〕n. 歷史
interesting〔'ɪntrɪstɪŋ〕adj. 有趣的　　story〔'storɪ〕n. 故事

2. *I like collecting cards*.

collect〔kəˈlɛkt〕v. 收集　　card〔kɑrd〕n. 卡片

這句話的意思是「我喜歡收集卡片。」card 是作「卡片」解，在這裡可能包含很多種小朋友喜歡玩的卡片，像是遊戲卡、球員卡、怪獸卡等等。這句話還可以說成：I enjoy card collecting. (我喜歡收集卡片。)

3. *I like being outdoors*.

be〔bi〕v. 在；位於 (being〔ˈbiɪŋ〕be 的動名詞)
outdoors〔ˈaʊtˈdorz〕adv. 在戶外

這句話的意思是「我喜歡待在戶外。」也可以說成：I like to be outdoors. (我喜歡待在戶外。) 或 I enjoy outdoor activities. (我喜歡戶外活動。)

outdoor〔ˈaʊtˌdor〕adj. 戶外的
activity〔ækˈtɪvətɪ〕n. 活動

being 也可以作「處於…的狀態」解。其用法舉例如下：

***Being* in love is a wonderful feeling.**
(戀愛是一種很棒的感覺。)

She thinks *being* single is better than being married. (她覺得單身比結婚好。)

wonderful〔ˈwʌndəfəl〕adj. 很棒的
feeling〔ˈfilɪŋ〕n. 感覺　　single〔ˈsɪŋgl〕adj. 單身的
married〔ˈmærɪd〕adj. 結婚的

4. ***Rollerblading is neat.***

rollerblading〔ˈrolɚˌbledɪŋ〕*n.* 溜直排輪

neat〔nit〕*adj.* 很棒的

這句話的意思是「溜直排輪很棒。」溜直排輪，比較正式的說法是：in-line skate，但是美國人比較常說 rollerblade，這個字原本是指美國最大的直排輪鞋公司，後來人們慢慢把這個字當成「溜直排輪」的意思。rollerblade 也可以當名詞用，就是「直排輪鞋」的意思。這句話也可以說成：Rollerblading is wonderful.（溜直排輪很棒。）

另外，neat 這個字的主要意思是「乾淨的；整潔的」，例如：Try to keep your room ***neat***.（試著讓你的房間保持乾淨。）但在這裡，是作「很棒的」（= *wonderful*）解，例如：

That was a ***neat*** party.（那是個很棒的宴會。）

I think action movies are so ***neat***.
（我覺得動作片很棒。）

Getting a red envelope on New Year's
　　Eve is ***neat***!
（在除夕夜拿到紅包，是一件很棒的事！）

party〔ˈpɑrtɪ〕*n.* 宴會　　action〔ˈækʃən〕*n.* 動作
movie〔ˈmuvɪ〕*n.* 電影　　red〔rɛd〕*adj.* 紅色的
envelope〔ˈɛnvəˌlop〕*n.* 信封　　***red envelope*** 紅包
New Year's Eve 除夕

5. ***In addition*, *I like to draw pictures*.**

in addition 另外　　draw〔drɔ〕*v.* 畫
picture〔'pɪktʃɚ〕*n.* 圖畫

　　　這句話的意思是「另外，我喜歡畫圖。」也有美國
人說：Also, I enjoy drawing.（另外，我喜歡畫畫。）
in addition 是副詞片語，作「另外；而且」（= *also*；
furthermore）解。例如：

***In addition*, I gave him my e-mail address.**
（另外，我把我的電郵地址給他。）

***In addition*, I bought some new shoes.**
（另外，我買了幾雙新鞋。）

e-mail〔'i,mel〕*n.* 電子郵件
address〔ə'drɛs〕*n.* 地址　　shoes〔ʃuz〕*n. pl.* 鞋子

　　　要特別注意的是，in addition 和 in addition to
意思不同，in addition to 是介系詞片語，後面須接
名詞或動名詞，作「除了…之外」解，例如：

***In addition to* Tai Chi, she also likes yoga.**
（除了太極拳之外，她還喜歡瑜珈。）

He speaks French *in addition to* English.
（除了英文之外，他還會說法文。）

Tai Chi〔'taɪ'dʒi〕*n.* 太極拳　　yoga〔'jogə〕*n.* 瑜珈
French〔frɛntʃ〕*n.* 法文

6. *Furthermore, I like music.*

furthermore〔'fɝðə͵mor〕*adv.* 此外；而且
music〔'mjuzɪk〕*n.* 音樂

　　這句話的意思是「而且，我喜歡音樂。」
furthermore 是作「此外；而且」(= *in addition*)
解，其用法舉例如下：

　　　　She is extremely smart; *furthermore*,
　　　　　she's very modest.
　　　　（她非常聰明，而且又很謙虛。）

　　　　He's the best student in his class;
　　　　　furthermore, he's a talented musician.
　　　　（他是他們班上最優秀的學生，而且他還是
　　　　　個很有才華的音樂家。）

　　　　extremely〔ɪk'strimlɪ〕*adv.* 非常
　　　　smart〔smart〕*adj.* 聰明的
　　　　modest〔'madɪst〕*adj.* 謙虛的
　　　　talented〔'tæləntɪd〕*adj.* 有才能的
　　　　musician〔mju'zɪʃən〕*n.* 音樂家

7. *I'm learning to play an instrument.*

learn〔lɝn〕*v.* 學習　　play〔ple〕*v.* 演奏
instrument〔'ɪnstrəmənt〕*n.* 樂器

　　play 的主要意思是「玩」，但在這裡是作「演奏」
(= *perform*) 解，所以這句話的意思是「我正在學習
演奏樂器。」美國人也常說：I'm studying an
instrument.（我正在學一種樂器。）

　　play 有很多種意思，須依前後文來判斷，下面是主要的意思：

① 作「演奏」解。

He often ***plays*** the piano after supper.
（他常在晚餐之後彈奏鋼琴。）

② 作「玩」解。

All children like to ***play*** with toys.
（所有的小孩都喜歡玩玩具。）

③ 作「打（球）」解。

My brother and I like to ***play*** basketball.
（我弟弟和我喜歡打籃球。）

piano〔pɪˈæno〕*n.* 鋼琴
supper〔ˈsʌpɚ〕*n.* 晚餐
toy〔tɔɪ〕*n.* 玩具
basketball〔ˈbæskɪtˌbɔl〕*n.* 籃球

8. ***Of course*, *I enjoy learning English.***

of course 當然　　enjoy〔ɪnˈdʒɔɪ〕*v.* 喜歡

　　這句話的意思是「當然，我也喜歡學英文。」of course 這個片語美國人天天都會用到，意思是「當然」（= *certainly*）。以下都是美國人常說的話：

***Of course*,** I love my parents!
（當然，我愛我的爸媽！）

***Of course*,** honesty is the best policy.
（當然，誠實為上策。）

【honesty〔ˈɑnɪstɪ〕*n.* 誠實　　policy〔ˈpɑləsɪ〕*n.* 政策】

○作文範例

My Hobbies

Everyone has different hobbies. Some people like to paint and others like to play basketball. I have many hobbies because I like to do many things. Let me share a few of my hobbies with you.

To begin with, I really like games, both indoor and outdoor. I like collecting cards and playing card games with my friends. But my favorite games are video games. I could play them all day long. *On the other hand*, I also like being outside in the fresh air and sunshine, so I play a lot of sports. I like bike riding and rollerblading very much, but swimming is my favorite sport.

In addition, I like to draw pictures and read comics, but please don't tell my parents because they don't approve. Listening to music and singing songs are things I enjoy too, and I'm learning how to play an instrument — the guitar. *Finally*, I enjoy learning English because I like speaking with foreigners and I like watching Disney cartoons.

As you can see, my hobbies keep me busy and excited. I'm always looking for new things to do!

● 中文翻譯

我 的 嗜 好

每個人都有不同的嗜好。有些人喜歡畫畫,而有些人喜歡打籃球。我有很多嗜好,因為我喜歡做的事很多。讓我告訴你們我的一些嗜好。

首先,我很喜歡玩遊戲,室內遊戲和戶外遊戲我都喜歡。我喜歡收集卡片,還有和朋友玩卡片的遊戲。但是我最喜歡的遊戲是電動玩具。我可以玩那個玩一整天。另一方面,我也喜歡待在有新鮮空氣和陽光的戶外,那我就可以從事很多運動。我很喜歡騎腳踏車兜風和溜直排輪,可是游泳是我最喜歡的運動。

另外,我喜歡畫圖和看漫畫,但是請不要告訴我爸媽,因為他們不准。聽音樂和唱歌也是我喜歡做的事,而且我還在學習演奏一種樂器 —— 吉他。最後,我喜歡學英文,因為我喜歡跟外國人講話,而且我喜歡看迪士尼卡通。

就如你所知,我的嗜好使我忙碌而興奮。我總是在找新的事情做!

3. My Family

3

I have a wonderful family.
I'm lucky to be a part of it.
Let me tell you about them.

My family name is Lee.
My family history is long and proud.
There are five people in my family now.

My parents love me very much.
They do a lot for me.
When I need help, they are always
   there.

family (ˈfæməlɪ)	wonderful (ˈwʌndəfəl)
lucky (ˈlʌkɪ)	part (part)
family name	history (ˈhɪstrɪ)
proud (praʊd)	parents (ˈpɛrənts)
always (ˈɔlwez)	there (ðɛr)

My dad is a strong guy.

He's honest and hardworking.

He's like a superhero to me.

My mom is a smart woman.

She can do almost anything.

I just can't praise her enough.

I have two siblings.

They are my older brother and
  younger sister.

Sometimes we argue, but we mainly
  get along.

---

strong〔strɔŋ〕   guy〔gaɪ〕

honest〔'anɪst〕

hardworking〔'hard,wɜkɪŋ〕

superhero〔'supə,hɪro〕

smart〔smart〕   woman〔'wʊmən〕

almost〔'ɔl,most〕   ***can't…enough***

praise〔prez〕   enough〔ə'nʌf〕

sibling〔'sɪblɪŋ〕   young〔jʌŋ〕

sometimes〔'sʌm,taɪmz〕   argue〔'argjʊ〕

mainly〔'menlɪ〕   ***get along***

***My family likes being together*.**

We like eating out and going to the
   movies.
We also enjoy hiking and having
   picnics.

3

My family isn't perfect.
We have our ups and downs.
But we always forgive and make up.

Our motto is "United together forever."
I'll always cherish my family.
I hope your family is lovely, too.

---

together (tə'gɛðɚ)   *eat out*
movie ('muvɪ)   *go to the movies*
enjoy (ɪn'dʒɔɪ)   hike (haɪk)
picnic ('pɪknɪk)   perfect ('pɜˑfɪkt)
ups and downs   forgive (fɚ'gɪv)
make up   motto ('mɑto)
united (ju'naɪtɪd)   forever (fɚ'ɛvɚ)
cherish ('tʃɛrɪʃ)   lovely ('lʌvlɪ)
too (tu)

3. My Family

● 演講解說

I have a wonderful family.   我有一個很棒的家庭。
I'm lucky to be a part of it.   我很幸運是它的一份子。
Let me tell you about them.   讓我告訴你們關於這個家的事。

My family name is Lee.   我姓李。
My family history is long
   and proud.   我的家族史非常悠久而且光榮。
There are five people in my
   family now.   我家現在有五個人。

My parents love me very
   much.   我的父母非常愛我。
They do a lot for me.   他們為我做了很多事。
When I need help, they are
   always there.   當我需要協助的時候,他們總
                              是在那裡。

** —————————————

family〔'fæməlɪ〕*n.* 家庭;家人
wonderful〔'wʌndɚfəl〕*adj.* 很棒的   lucky〔'lʌkɪ〕*adj.* 幸運的
part〔part〕*n.* 部分   *family name* 姓   history〔'hɪstrɪ〕*n.* 歷史
proud〔praud〕*adj.* 光榮的   parents〔'pɛrənts〕*n.pl.* 父母
always〔'ɔlwez〕*adv.* 總是;永遠地   there〔ðɛr〕*adv.* 在那裡

My dad is a strong guy.

He's honest and hardworking.

He's like a superhero to me.

我爸爸是個堅強的人。

他誠實而勤勉。

對我來說，他就像是超級英雄。

My mom is a smart woman.

She can do almost anything.

I just can't praise her enough.

我媽媽是個聰明的女人。

她幾乎會做任何事。

我就是再怎麼稱讚她也不爲過。

I have two siblings.

They are my older brother
   and younger sister.

Sometimes we argue, but we
   mainly get along.

我有兩個兄弟姊妹。

他們是我的哥哥和妹妹。

我們有時會吵架，但是大部分
的時候都處得很好。

**

strong〔strɔŋ〕*adj.* 堅強的；強壯的　　guy〔gaɪ〕*n.* (男)人

honest〔'ɑnɪst〕*adj.* 誠實的

hardworking〔'hɑrd,wɜkɪŋ〕*adj.* 勤勉的

superhero〔'supɚ,hɪro〕*n.* 超級英雄

smart〔smɑrt〕*adj.* 聰明的　　woman〔'wʊmən〕*n.* 女人

almost〔'ɔl,most〕*adv.* 幾乎　　***can't…enough*** 再…也不爲過

praise〔prez〕*v.* 稱讚；讚美　　enough〔ə'nʌf〕*adv.* 足夠地

sibling〔'sɪblɪŋ〕*n.* 兄弟姊妹　　young〔jʌŋ〕*adj.* 年輕的

sometimes〔'sʌm,taɪmz〕*adv.* 有時　　argue〔'ɑrgju〕*v.* 爭吵

mainly〔'menlɪ〕*adv.* 大部分　　***get along*** 相處；處得好

My family likes being together.	我的家人喜歡聚在一起。
We like eating out and going to the movies.	我們喜歡出去吃飯和看電影。
We also enjoy hiking and having picnics.	我們還喜歡健行和野餐。
My family isn't perfect.	我的家庭並不是完美無缺的。
We have our ups and downs.	我們的關係起起伏伏。
But we always forgive and make up.	但是我們一定會原諒對方並和好。
Our motto is "United together forever."	我們的座右銘是「永遠團結在一起」。
I'll always cherish my family.	我會永遠珍惜我的家庭。
I hope your family is lovely, too.	我希望你的家庭也一樣可愛。

3

** ————————————————

together〔tə'gɛðɚ〕*adv.* 一起　　***eat out*** 外出用餐

movie〔'muvɪ〕*n.* 電影　　***go to the movies*** 去看電影

enjoy〔ɪn'dʒɔɪ〕*v.* 喜歡　　hike〔haɪk〕*v.* 健行

picnic〔'pɪknɪk〕*n.* 野餐　　perfect〔'pɝfɪkt〕*adj.* 完美的

ups and downs 起伏；變動　　forgive〔fɚ'gɪv〕*v.* 原諒

make up 和好　　motto〔'mɑto〕*n.* 座右銘

united〔ju'naɪtɪd〕*adj.* 團結的

forever〔fɚ'ɛvɚ〕*adv.* 永遠　　cherish〔'tʃɛrɪʃ〕*v.* 珍惜

lovely〔'lʌvlɪ〕*adj.* 可愛的；美好的　　too〔tu〕*adv.* 也

● 背景說明

　　家庭對每個小朋友來說，都非常重要。本篇演講稿要教大家，如何介紹自己的家庭，試著把爸媽和兄弟姊妹的優點告訴所有人，在這樣做的過程中，你將學會欣賞和珍惜你的家人。

3

1. *Let me tell you about them.*

　　這句話的意思是「讓我告訴你們關於這個家的事。」一般的動詞，後面要再接一個動詞時，中間都要加 to，例如：I want to go to school.（我要去上學。）但是，let 這個字是使役動詞，所以後面須接原形動詞。

　　　　　She *let* me <u>hold</u> her hand.
　　　　　　　　　　 原形動詞
　　　　　（她讓我牽她的手。）

　　　　　Let everyone <u>know</u> the good news.
　　　　　　　　　　　 原形動詞
　　　　　（讓大家都知道這個好消息。）

　　　　　hold〔hold〕*v.* 捉住；握
　　　　　news〔njuz〕*n.* 消息；新聞

　　相同用法的使役動詞，還有 make、have、bid（命令），你只要記住，當你要使喚別人時，口氣通常會比較急迫，所以會省略 to，直接加原形動詞，好儘快告訴別人你要他做的事。【bid〔bɪd〕*v.* 命令】

3

2. *My family name is Lee.*

family name 姓

　　這句話的意思是「我姓李。」family name 就是「家族姓氏」的意思，這個字可能是源自歐洲中古時期，在一個莊園裡，上從地主，下至奴隸，全部都要沿用地主的姓氏，所以到後來，family name 就變成「姓」的意思了。

　　另外，family name 還等於 surname 和 last name。surname 是比較正式的用法，平常不常用，但是會出現在一些表格上，所以當你下次填表，看到 surname 時，就只要把姓填上去就可以了。而「名字」則是 first name 或 given name。【surname〔'sɝ͵nem〕n. 姓】

3. *There are five people in my family now.*

　　這句話的意思是「我家現在有五個人。」there are 是「有」的意思，如果是單數，就用 there is。要告訴別人你家有幾個人，還可以這樣說：

My family has five people.（我家有五個人。）
【有些人會說，這種說法是錯的，但是其實美國人常這樣說。】

There are five members in my family.
（我家有五位成員。）【member〔'mɛmbɚ〕n. 成員】
【這句話雖然正確，但美國人較少用。】

3

4. *My dad is a strong guy.*

dad〔dæd〕*n.* 爸爸　　strong〔strɔŋ〕*adj.* 堅強的
guy〔gaɪ〕*n.*（男）人

　　strong 的主要意思是「強壯的」，這個字可以用來形容身體強壯，或是堅強的心靈，所以這句話的意思是「我爸爸是個堅強的人。」也可以說成：

My father is a capable guy.
（我父親是個能幹的人。）

My pop is a tough man.
（我爸是個堅強的男人。）

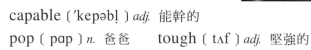

capable〔'kepəbl〕*adj.* 能幹的
pop〔pɑp〕*n.* 爸爸　　tough〔tʌf〕*adj.* 堅強的

　　guy 是「男人；人」的意思，等於 man、fellow 或 person。當你指一個男生可以用 guy，一群人裡面，有男有女時，可以用 guys。特別注意，兩個以上的女生在一起的時候，也可以用 guys，只有一個女生時，就不能用 guy，只能用 girl 或 miss。如：Excuse me, miss.（對不起，小姐。）
【fellow〔'fɛlo〕*n.* 傢伙；人　　miss〔mɪs〕*n.* 小姐】

　　guy 的用法舉例如下：

You *guys* are too noisy.（你們太吵了。）

Every movie has both good *guys* and
　bad *guys* in it.
（每一部電影裡，都有好人和壞人。）
【noisy〔'nɔɪzɪ〕*adj.* 吵鬧的】

5. *I just can't praise her enough.*

can't…enough 再…也不爲過；…不盡
praise〔prez〕*v.* 稱讚　　enough〔ə'nʌf〕*adv.* 足夠地

　　這句話的意思是「我就是再怎麼稱讚她也不爲過。」
can't…enough 就是「再…也不爲過；…不盡」，enough
通常都放在句尾，例如：

I *can't* thank you *enough*.
（我對你感激不盡。）

You *can't* be careful *enough*.
（你再怎麼小心都不爲過。）

The steak is delicious.　I *can't* get *enough*.
（牛排眞好吃。我欲罷不能。）

careful〔'kɛrfəl〕*adj.* 小心的　　steak〔stek〕*n.* 牛排
delicious〔dɪ'lɪʃəs〕*adj.* 好吃的　　get〔gɛt〕*v.* 吃

6. *Sometimes we argue, but we mainly get along.*

sometimes〔'sʌm,taɪmz〕*adv.* 有時
argue〔'ɑrgjʊ〕*v.* 爭吵　　mainly〔'menlɪ〕*adv.* 大部分
get along 相處；處得好

　　這句話的意思是「我們有時會吵架，但是大部分的
時候都處得很好。」mainly 就是「大部分」的意思，
等於 most of the time（大部分的時候）或 mostly
（大部分地），所以這句話也可以說成：We sometimes
quarrel, but we mostly get along.
　【quarrel〔'kwɑrəl〕*v.* 吵架】

7. *We have our ups and downs.*

　　ups and downs 　起伏；變動

　　　　這句話字面的意思是「我們有我們的起伏。」引申為「我們的關係起起伏伏。」沒有一個家庭是永遠都不吵架的，和家人朝夕相處，難免有摩擦，唯有懂得放寬心胸，原諒對方的人，才能擁有美滿的家庭。

　　這句話還可以説成：

3

　　　　Our relationship has its good times and
　　　　　　its bad times. (我們的關係時好時壞。)

　　　　We don't always get along.
　　　　(我們不一定處得很好。)

　　　　relationship〔rɪ'leʃən,ʃɪp〕*n.* 關係
　　　　not always 　未必；不一定
　　　　get along 　相處；處得好

　　　　ups and downs 是「起伏；變動」的意思
　　(= *happy and unhappy experiences ; happy and*
　　sad times)。例如：

　　　　Life is full of *ups and downs*.
　　　　(人生起起伏伏。)

　　　　【這句話一定要背下來，這是美國人很常講的話，
　　　　　寫英文作文時，一定能派上用場。】

　　　　All people have their *ups and downs*.
　　　　(每個人都有快樂和悲傷的時刻。)

8. ***But we always forgive and make up.***

forgive〔fɚˋgɪv〕v. 原諒　　***make up*** 和好

　　　　這句話的意思是「但是我們一定會原諒對方並和好。」家人是一輩子陪在你身邊的人，所以當他們犯錯時，你一定要和他們和好，俗話說得好：「家和萬事興。」擁有和樂的家庭，你才能放心追求自己的夢想。

　　　　make up 有很多種意思，必須依前後句意來判斷，下面是主要的意思：

① 作「和好」解。

After quarreling, the couple kissed and ***made up***.（吵完架之後，這對夫婦接吻，然後就和好了。）

② 作「組成」解。

This team is ***made up*** of eight boys.
（這支隊伍是由八個男孩所組成的。）

③ 作「化妝」解。

It takes her about twenty minutes to ***make up*** her face every day.
（她每天大約花二十分鐘來化妝。）

④ 作「編造」解。

He always ***makes up*** excuses for being late.
（他總是為自己的遲到找藉口。）

quarrel〔ˋkwɑrəl〕v. 爭吵　　couple〔ˋkʌpl〕n. 夫婦
kiss〔kɪs〕v. 親吻　　team〔tim〕n. 隊伍
about〔əˋbaʊt〕adv. 大約　　minute〔ˋmɪnɪt〕n. 分鐘
excuse〔ɪkˋskjus〕n. 藉口　　late〔let〕adj. 遲到的

● 作文範例

My Family

A family is very important. You can always count on your family to give you love and support. I love my family very much, and now I would like to introduce them to you.

My family name is Lee. There are five people in my family. My parents are great. When I need help, they are always there for me. My dad is strong, honest and very hardworking. He is somebody you can count on. My mom is great, too! She can do almost anything. I also have an older brother and a younger sister. We usually get along okay. We like doing things together. We enjoy hiking, going on picnics and going to the movies together. That's an introduction to my family. I hope your family is as nice as mine.

● 中文翻譯

我 的 家 庭

家庭非常重要。你可以一直靠你的家人給你愛和支持。我非常愛我的家庭，我現在想要把我的家人介紹給你。

我姓李。我家有五個人。我的父母很偉大。當我需要幫助時，他們總是在那裡等著幫我。我爸爸堅強、誠實，而且非常勤快。他是個你可以依賴的人。我媽媽也很偉大！她幾乎會做任何事。我還有一個哥哥和妹妹。我們通常都處得不錯。我們喜歡一起做事。我們喜歡健行、野餐，還有一起去看電影。這就是我對我們家的介紹。我希望你的家庭也跟我的一樣好。

4. My Best Friend

I have a best friend.
We met at school.
We're in the same grade.

He's a diligent student.
He's very hardworking.
I learn a lot from him.

He helps me with math.
I help him with English.
We're a good study team.

---

best (bɛst)   friend (frɛnd)

meet (mit)   same (sem)

grade (gred)

diligent ('dɪlədʒənt)

hardworking ('hɑrd,wɜkɪŋ)   math (mæθ)

study ('stʌdɪ)   team (tim)

He's honest and reliable.

I trust him completely.

We share secrets all the time.

He's loyal and brave.

Once a bully teased me.

He came to my rescue right away.

4

He's considerate and polite.

He makes me little gifts.

He always remembers my birthday.

honest ('anɪst)　　　reliable (rɪ'laɪəbl̩)

trust (trʌst)　　　completely (kəm'plitlɪ)

share (ʃɛr)　　　secret ('sikrɪt)

all the time　　　loyal ('lɔɪəl)

brave (brev)　　　once (wʌns)

bully ('bʊlɪ)　　　tease (tiz)

rescue ('rɛskju)　　　*come to one's rescue*

right away　　　considerate (kən'sɪdərɪt)

polite (pə'laɪt)　　　little ('lɪtl̩)

gift (gɪft)　　　remember (rɪ'mɛmbɚ)

birthday ('bɝθ,de)

He is fun to be with.

He tells funny jokes.

His stories make me laugh.

He's a good listener.

He knows when I'm blue.

He picks me up when I'm down.

He's one of a kind.

We'll stay friends forever.

I hope you have a friend like mine.

4

---

fun〔fʌn〕	with〔wɪθ〕
funny〔'fʌnɪ〕	joke〔dʒok〕
laugh〔læf〕	listener〔'lɪsn̩ɚ〕
blue〔blu〕	**pick** *sb*. **up**
down〔daʊn〕	kind〔kaɪnd〕
one of a kind	stay〔ste〕
forever〔fɚ'ɛvɚ〕	hope〔hop〕
mine〔maɪn〕	

4. My Best Friend

● 演講解說

I have a best friend.　　　　　我有一個最要好的朋友。

We met at school.　　　　　　我們是在學校認識的。

We're in the same grade.　　　　我們是同一年級的。

He's a diligent student.　　　　他是個用功的學生。

He's very hardworking.　　　　他非常勤勉。

I learn a lot from him.　　　　　我從他身上學到很多。

He helps me with math.　　　　他幫我學數學。

I help him with English.　　　　我幫他學英文。

We're a good study team.　　　　我們是很棒的學習團隊。

** ————————————————————

best〔bɛst〕*adj.* 最好的　　friend〔frɛnd〕*n.* 朋友

meet〔mit〕*v.* 認識　　same〔sem〕*adj.* 相同的

grade〔gred〕*n.* 年級

diligent〔'dɪlədʒənt〕*adj.* 勤勉的；用功的

hardworking〔'hard͵wɜkɪŋ〕*adj.* 勤勉的　　math〔mæθ〕*n.* 數學

study〔'stʌdɪ〕*n.* 讀書；學習　　team〔tim〕*n.* 團隊

He's honest and reliable.	他誠實又可靠。
I trust him completely.	我完全信任他。
We share secrets all the time.	我們總是把秘密告訴對方。
He's loyal and brave.	他忠實而勇敢。
Once a bully teased me.	曾經有個惡霸欺負我。
He came to my rescue right away.	他馬上就來救我。
He's considerate and polite.	他體貼而且有禮貌。
He makes me little gifts.	他會做小禮物送我。
He always remembers my birthday.	他總是記得我的生日。

4

** ————————————————

honest〔ˈɑnɪst〕*adj.* 誠實的　　reliable〔rɪˈlaɪəbl̩〕*adj.* 可靠的

trust〔trʌst〕*v.* 信任　　completely〔kəmˈplitlɪ〕*adv.* 完全地

share〔ʃɛr〕*v.* 分享；告訴　　secret〔ˈsikrɪt〕*n.* 秘密

all the time 經常；總是　　loyal〔ˈlɔɪəl〕*adj.* 忠實的

brave〔brev〕*adj.* 勇敢的　　once〔wʌns〕*adv.* 從前；曾經

bully〔ˈbulɪ〕*n.* (在學校裡) 欺負弱者的學生；惡霸

tease〔tiz〕*v.* 戲弄；欺負　　rescue〔ˈrɛskju〕*n.* 解救

come to *one's* ***rescue*** 去解救某人；對某人伸出援手

right away 馬上；立刻　　considerate〔kənˈsɪdərɪt〕*adj.* 體貼的

polite〔pəˈlaɪt〕*adj.* 有禮貌的　　little〔ˈlɪtl̩〕*adj.* 小的

gift〔gɪft〕*n.* 禮物　　remember〔rɪˈmɛmbɚ〕*v.* 記得

birthday〔ˈbɝθ,de〕*n.* 生日

He is fun to be with.	跟他在一起很有趣。
He tells funny jokes.	他會講好笑的笑話。
His stories make me laugh.	他的故事使我哈哈大笑。
He's a good listener.	他是個很棒的聽衆。
He knows when I'm blue.	他知道我什麼時候憂鬱。
He picks me up when I'm down.	當我沮喪時，他會使我振作。
He's one of a kind.	他是獨一無二的。
We'll stay friends forever.	我們會永遠做朋友。
I hope you have a friend like mine.	我希望你也像我一樣，有一個這樣的朋友。

4

** ————————————

fun〔fʌn〕*adj.* 有趣的　　with〔wɪθ〕*prep.* 與⋯一起
funny〔'fʌnɪ〕*adj.* 好笑的　　joke〔dʒok〕*n.* 笑話
laugh〔læf〕*v.* 笑　　listener〔'lɪsn̩ɚ〕*n.* 聽衆；傾聽者
blue〔blu〕*adj.* 憂鬱的　　*pick sb. up* 使某人振作起來
down〔daʊn〕*adj.* 沮喪的　　kind〔kaɪnd〕*n.* 種類
one of a kind 獨一無二的　　stay〔ste〕*v.* 繼續是
forever〔fə'ɛvɚ〕*adv.* 永遠　　hope〔hop〕*v.* 希望
mine〔maɪn〕*pron.* 我的（東西）

背景說明

　　每個人都有很多朋友，但是最要好的朋友，通常只有一、兩個。你最要好的朋友了解你的一切，他會與你分享快樂與悲傷，當你需要他的時候，他一定會陪伴在你身邊。這個朋友對你而言如此重要，你當然要學會用英文來介紹他。

4

1. ***We met at school.***

　　meet〔mit〕*v.* 認識

　　　　meet 的基本意思是「會面」，例如：They often ***met*** each other.（他們常常見面。）但在本句中，meet 是作「認識」解。at school 也可說成 in school，兩者使用頻率相同。以下都是美國人常說的話，我們依照使用頻率排列：

　　① ***We met at school.***【第一常用】
　　　　（我們是在學校認識的。）

　　② We first met each other in school.
　　　　（我們第一次見到對方，是在學校裡。）【第二常用】

　　③ We became friends in school.【第三常用】
　　　　（我們是在學校變成朋友的。）

　　④ We got to know each other in school.
　　　　（我們是在學校認識彼此的。）

each other 彼此；互相　　become〔bɪˈkʌm〕*v.* 變成
get to V. 得以～；能夠～

2. ***He helps me with math.***
I help him with English.

math〔mæθ〕*n.* 數學

這兩句話的意思是「他幫我學數學。我幫他學英文。」美國人也常說：We help each other with our schoolwork. (我們在課業方面互相幫忙。)

【schoolwork〔'skul,wɜk〕*n.* 課業】

當你要說明「幫忙某人做某事」時，就用 ***help sb. with*** *sth.* 這個句型，例如：

The accountant ***helped*** him ***with*** the tax return.
(會計師協助他報稅的事。)

My best friend always ***helps*** me ***with*** my
problems. (我最好的朋友總是會幫我解決問題。)

accountant〔ə'kauntənt〕*n.* 會計師
tax〔tæks〕*n.* 稅　　return〔rɪ'tɜn〕*n.* 申報 (書)

3. ***Once a bully teased me.***

once〔wʌns〕*adv.* 從前；曾經
bully〔'bulɪ〕*n.* (在學校裡) 欺負弱者的學生；惡霸
tease〔tiz〕*v.* 戲弄；欺負

這句話的意思是「曾經有個惡霸欺負我。」once 放在句首，是當副詞用，作「從前；曾經」解，等於 one time 或 at one time。例如：***Once*** there was a witch who lived in the village. (從前村裡住了一個巫婆。)

【witch〔wɪtʃ〕*n.* 巫婆　　village〔'vɪlɪdʒ〕*n.* 村莊】

這句話也可以說成：

Once a really rude guy mocked me.

（從前有個非常無禮的人嘲弄我。）

One time a mean person ridiculed me.

（有一次有個卑鄙的人嘲笑我。）

really〔'rilɪ〕adv. 非常地　　rude〔rud〕adj. 無禮的
guy〔gaɪ〕n. 人；傢伙
mock〔mɑk〕v. 嘲笑；愚弄
time〔taɪm〕n. 次　　mean〔min〕adj. 卑鄙的
ridicule〔'rɪdɪkjul〕v. 嘲笑

4

4. ***He came to my rescue right away.***

rescue〔'rɛskju〕v., n. 解救；援救
come to one's ***rescue*** 去解救某人；對某人伸出援手
right away 馬上；立刻

　　rescue 這個字，可當名詞或動詞用，在此是名詞，作「援救」解。而 come to one's rescue 字面的意思是「前來援救」，也就是「去解救某人」，例如：The army ***came to*** the flood victims' ***rescue***.（軍隊去救水災的受害者。）

army〔'ɑrmɪ〕n. 軍隊
flood〔flʌd〕n. 水災
victim〔'vɪktɪm〕n. 受害者

這句話的意思是「他馬上就來救我。」以下都是
美國人常説的話：

① *He came to my rescue right away*.【第一常用】
（他馬上就來救我。）

② He immediately helped me out.【第二常用】
（他立刻來幫我。）

③ He quickly came to my assistance.
（他很快就來幫我。）【第三常用】

④ He helped me without delay.
（他馬上來幫我。）

immediately〔ɪ'midɪɪtlɪ〕*adv.* 立刻

help sb. out 幫忙某人　　quickly〔'kwɪklɪ〕*adv.* 快地

assistance〔ə'sɪstəns〕*n.* 幫助

come to one's *assistance* 幫助某人

without〔wɪð'aut〕*prep.* 沒有　　delay〔dɪ'le〕*n.* 延遲

without delay 立刻；馬上

5. *He is fun to be with*.

fun〔fʌn〕*adj.* 有趣的　　with〔wɪθ〕*prep.* 與…一起

這句話的意思是「跟他在一起很有趣。」這句話是
對朋友最好的稱讚。另外，你還可以說：He's a good
time.（跟他在一起很開心。）意思是：He always gives
me a good time when I'm with him.（當我跟他在一
起時，他總是讓我擁有美好的時光。）這兩句都是老外常
講的話，如果你也這樣説，他們就會覺得你的英文很好。

6. *He knows when I'm blue.*

blue〔blu〕*adj.* 憂鬱的

　　　　blue 這個字原本是「藍色」的意思，而 blues 原本是指黑人爵士樂曲—藍調（又稱布魯士），這種音樂的曲風憂鬱，所以後來 blues 就引申有「憂鬱」的意思，是名詞，而 blue 則是形容詞，作「憂鬱的」解。

　　　　這句話的意思是「他知道我什麼時候憂鬱。」也可以說成：He understands my moods.（他了解我的心情。）【understand〔͵ʌndɚˋstænd〕*v.* 了解 mood〔mud〕*n.* 心情】

4

7. *He picks me up when I'm down.*

pick sb. up　使某人振作起來　　down〔daʊn〕*adj.* 沮喪的

　　　　down 的主要意思是「在下面」，是當副詞用，但在這裡，down 是當形容詞用，作「沮喪的」解。這句話的意思是「當我沮喪時，他會使我振作。」也可以說成：When I'm sad, he cheers me up.（當我悲傷時，他會讓我開心。）

sad〔sæd〕*adj.* 悲傷的

cheer sb. up　使某人高興

　　pick up 這個片語有很多種用法，要依照前後文來判斷意思，例如：

　　① 作「使振作起來」解。

　　　　He picks me up when I'm down.

　　　　（當我沮喪時，他會使我振作。）

② 作「撿起來」解。

Always *pick up* garbage whenever you see it.
（每當你看到垃圾時，一定要撿起來。）

③ 作「搭載」解。

My mom *picks* me *up* after school on rainy
    days.（在下雨天的時候，我媽放學後會來載我。）

④ 作「學習」解，指「沒有人教，自然學會」，
像「撿起來」一樣。

4

She *picked up* driving in a week.
（她在一個星期之內學會開車。）

garbage〔'gɑrbɪdʒ〕*n.* 垃圾
whenever〔hwɛn'ɛvə〕*conj.* 每當
rainy〔'renɪ〕*adj.* 下雨的   driving〔'draɪvɪŋ〕*n.* 開車

8. *He's one of a kind*.
kind〔kaɪnd〕*n.* 種類   *one of a kind* 獨一無二的

這句話的意思是「他是獨一無二的。」one of a
kind 的字面意思是「同類中唯一的一個」（詳見「一口
氣英語②」p.6-5），引申作「獨一無二的；非常特別的」
解，類似的說法還有：

He is one in a million.（他非常優秀。）
He is unique.（他很獨特。）
There is no one like him.（沒有人像他一樣。）

million〔'mɪljən〕*n.* 百萬
in a million（一百萬個中只有一個）罕見的；極優秀的
unique〔ju'nik〕*adj.* 獨特的   like〔laɪk〕*prep.* 像

○ 作文範例

My Best Friend

Everybody has a best friend that they can share everything with. I also have a best friend. We met in school, and we're in the same grade.

My best friend is a good student because he is very hardworking. I learn a lot from him. He helps me with math; I help him with English. We always help each other. Besides that, he's honest and reliable. I trust him completely and we share secrets all the time.

My best friend is also loyal and brave. Once when a bully teased me, he came to my rescue right away. He always remembers my birthday and he is fun to be with. He tells funny jokes and stories. He always makes me laugh. Finally, he is a very good listener and he knows how to cheer me up when I'm down.

My best friend is really one of a kind. I hope we'll stay friends forever.

4

● 中文翻譯

我最要好的朋友

　　每個人都有一個最要好的朋友，可以分享一切。我也有一個最要好的朋友。我們是在學校認識的，而且我們唸同一個年級。

　　我最要好的朋友是個好學生，因為他非常勤勉。我從他身上學到很多。他幫我學數學；我幫他學英文。我們總是互相幫忙。此外，他誠實又可靠。我完全信任他，而且我們總是把秘密告訴對方。

　　我最好的朋友也很忠實和勇敢。曾經有個惡霸欺負我，他馬上就來救我。他總是記得我的生日，而且跟他在一起很有趣。他會講有趣的笑話和故事。他總是使我哈哈大笑。最後，他是個很棒的聽眾，當我沮喪時，他知道如何使我振作。

　　我最要好的朋友真的是獨一無二的。我希望我們永遠是朋友。

5. My Daily Schedule

My day is typical.
I bet it's like yours.
Let me tell you my routine.

My alarm goes off at 6:30.
I take my time getting up.
I rise and shine with a stretch.

5

I take off my PJ's.
I wash up quickly.
I brush my teeth and comb my hair.

daily (ˈdelɪ)	schedule (ˈskɛdʒul)
typical (ˈtɪpɪkl̩)	*I bet*
routine (ruˈtin)	alarm (əˈlɑrm)
go off	*take one's time*
get up	shine (ʃaɪn)
rise and shine	stretch (strɛtʃ)
take off	*PJ's*
wash up	quickly (ˈkwɪklɪ)
brush (brʌʃ)	comb (kom)

I put on my uniform.

I pack my backpack for school.

Then, I put on my sneakers and leave.

I never skip breakfast.

I eat at home or on the way.

But I always eat in a hurry.

After school, I go to a cram school.

I hit the books again there.

I finish my homework for the day.

put on	uniform〔'junə,fɔrm〕
pack〔pæk〕	backpack〔'bæk,pæk〕
then〔ðɛn〕	sneakers〔'snikəz〕
skip〔skɪp〕	*on the way*
in a hurry	*cram school*
hit the books	finish〔'fɪnɪʃ〕
for the day	

Finally, I return home.

I relax and take a break.

I have dinner with my family.

I watch some TV.

I go to bed around 9:30.

I fall asleep right away.

On weekends, everything is different.

I sleep late and have a ball.

Is your day the same as mine?

5

---

finally ('faɪnḷɪ)

relax (rɪ'læks)

dinner ('dɪnɚ)

around (ə'raʊnd)

fall asleep

weekend ('wik'ɛnd)

sleep (slip)

have a ball

mine (maɪn)

return (rɪ'tɝn)

break (brek)

go to bed

asleep (ə'slip)

right away

different ('dɪfərənt)

late (let)

the same as

5. My Daily Schedule

◎演講解說

My day is typical.	我過著一般人過的日子。
I bet it's like yours.	我確信我過的日子就跟你們一樣。
Let me tell you my routine.	讓我告訴你們我每天都會做的事。
My alarm goes off at 6:30.	我的鬧鐘六點半響。
I take my time getting up.	我從容地起床。
I rise and shine with a stretch.	我醒來以後，會伸個懶腰。
I take off my PJ's.	我會脫掉睡衣。
I wash up quickly.	我會很快地洗把臉。
I brush my teeth and comb my hair.	我會刷牙和梳頭髮。

**

daily〔'delɪ〕*adj.* 日常的　　schedule〔'skɛdʒul〕*n.* 時間表

typical〔'tɪpɪkl̩〕*adj.* 典型的；平凡的　　*I bet* 我敢打賭；我確信

routine〔ru'tin〕*n.* 例行公事　　alarm〔ə'lɑrm〕*n.* 鬧鐘

go off（鬧鐘）響　　*take one's time* 慢慢地　　*get up* 起床

rise and shine 醒來；起床　　stretch〔strɛtʃ〕*n.* 伸懶腰

take off 脫掉　　*PJ's* 睡衣（= *pajamas*）　　*wash up* 洗臉

brush〔brʌʃ〕*v.* 刷　　comb〔kom〕*v.* 梳

I put on my uniform.

I pack my backpack for
　　school.

Then, I put on my sneakers
　　and leave.

I never skip breakfast.

I eat at home or on the way.

But I always eat in a hurry.

After school, I go to a cram
　　school.

I hit the books again there.

I finish my homework for
　　the day.

| |
我穿上制服。

我把上學要用的東西裝進
背包。

然後，我穿上運動鞋出門。

我從來不會不吃早餐。

我會在家裡吃，或是在上學
的途中吃。

但我總是吃得很急。

放學後，我會去補習班。

我在那裡再用功唸一次書。

我會把當天的家庭作業寫完。

5

** ————————————

put on 穿上　　uniform〔'junəˌfɔrm〕*n.* 制服

pack〔pæk〕*v.* 把東西裝進…　　backpack〔'bækˌpæk〕*n.* 背包

school〔skul〕*n.* 上學　　sneakers〔'snikəz〕*n. pl.* 運動鞋

leave〔liv〕*v.* 離開　　skip〔skɪp〕*v.* 省去（某餐）不吃

on the way 在途中　　***in a hurry*** 匆忙地

after school 放學後　　***cram school*** 補習班

hit the books 用功唸書

finish〔'fɪnɪʃ〕*v.* 完成　　***for the day*** 一天的

Finally, *I return home*.	最後，我會回到家。
I relax and take a break.	我會放輕鬆，然後休息一下。
I have dinner with my family.	我會和我的家人一起吃晚餐。
I watch some TV.	我會看一下電視。
I go to bed around 9:30.	我大約九點半上床睡覺。
I fall asleep right away.	我會馬上睡著。
On weekends, everything is different.	在週末，每件事都會不一樣。
I sleep late and have a ball.	我會睡到很晚，而且玩得很痛快。
Is your day the same as mine?	你也過著和我一樣的日子嗎？

5

** ─────────────

finally〔ˈfaɪnḷɪ〕*adv.* 最後　　return〔rɪˈtɜn〕*v.* 返回
relax〔rɪˈlæks〕*v.* 放鬆　　break〔brek〕*n.* 休息時間
take a break 休息一下　　dinner〔ˈdɪnɚ〕*n.* 晚餐
go to bed 就寢；上床睡覺　　around〔əˈraʊnd〕*prep.* 大約
asleep〔əˈslip〕*adj.* 睡著的　　*fall asleep* 睡著
right away 馬上　　weekend〔ˈwikˈɛnd〕*n.* 週末
different〔ˈdɪfərənt〕*adj.* 不一樣的　　sleep〔slip〕*v.* 睡
late〔let〕*adv.* 晚　　*have a ball* 玩得痛快
the same as 和～相同　　mine〔maɪn〕*pron.* 我的（東西）

背景說明

　　從星期一到星期五，每個小朋友都要早早起床去上學，放學之後，可能是直接回家，也可能是到補習班去補習或唸書。本篇演講稿，要教你用英文來介紹自己的日常生活作息，讓大家更了解你。

1. *My day is typical.*

    day〔de〕*n.* 日子　　typical〔'tɪpɪkḷ〕*adj.* 典型的；平凡的

    　　typical 的主要意思是「典型的」，但在這裡是作「普通的；平凡的」解 (= *usual*)。所以，這句話的意思是「我過著平凡的日子。」也就是「我過著一般人過的日子。」還可以說成：My day is very ordinary. (我過的日子很普通。)【ordinary〔'ɔrdṇˌɛrɪ〕*adj.* 普通的】

2. *I bet it's like yours.*

    bet〔bɛt〕*v.* 打賭　　*I bet* 我敢打賭；我確信
    like〔laɪk〕*prep.* 像　　yours〔jʊrz〕*pron.* 你的 (東西)

    　　這句話的意思是「我確信我過的日子就跟你們一樣。」(= *I'm pretty sure it's like yours.*) 中國人常說「我打賭」或是「我跟你打賭」，這通常表示我們對某件事很有把握，而老外的說法，就是 I bet，例如：*I bet* she will agree. (我確信她會同意。) *I bet* 等於 *I'm pretty sure* (我確信)。

    pretty〔'prɪtɪ〕*adv.* 非常　　sure〔ʃʊr〕*adj.* 確信的
    agree〔ə'gri〕*v.* 同意

5

3. ***My alarm goes off at 6:30***.

alarm〔ə'lɑrm〕*n.* 鬧鐘 (= *alarm clock*)
go off (鬧鐘、警報器等)響

這句話的意思是「我的鬧鐘六點半響。」也可以
說成：

My alarm clock rings at 6:30
   every morning.

(我的鬧鐘每天早上六點半響。)

【ring〔rɪŋ〕*v.* (鈴) 響】

go off 有很多種意思，必須依前後句意來判斷：

① 作「(鬧鐘、警報器等)響」(= *ring*) 解。

The smoke made the fire alarm ***go off***.
   (煙霧使得火災警報器開始響。)

② 作「爆炸」(= *explode*) 解。

The bomb ***went off*** outside the police
   station. (炸彈在警察局外面爆炸。)

③ 作「關掉；熄滅」(= *turn off*) 解。

The street lights ***go off*** at 5:30 A.M.
   (街燈在早上五點半熄滅。)

smoke〔smok〕*n.* 煙霧   ***fire alarm*** 火災警報器
bomb〔bɑm〕*n.* 炸彈
outside〔'aʊt'saɪd〕*prep.* 在…外面
police station 警察局   street〔strit〕*n.* 街道
light〔laɪt〕*n.* 燈   ***A.M.*** 上午

4. *I take my time getting up*.

　　take one's time 從容地；慢慢地　　*get up* 起床

　　　　這句話的意思是「我從容地起床。」也可以說成：I get up slowly. (我慢慢地起床。)

　　　　take one's time 是作「從容地；慢慢地」解，例如：

> Always *take your time* when you make
> 　important decisions.
> (當你做重要決定時，一定要慢慢來。)

> Older people like to *take their time* when
> 　they do things. (老人家做事喜歡慢慢來。)
>
> important〔ɪmˈpɔrtn̩t〕*adj.* 重要的
> decision〔dɪˈsɪʒən〕*n.* 決定　　old〔old〕*adj.* 年老的

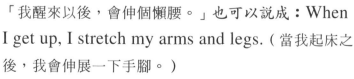

5. *I rise and shine with a stretch*.

　　rise and shine 醒來；起床
　　stretch〔strɛtʃ〕*n., v.* 伸展 (四肢)；伸懶腰

　　　　rise and shine 原本可能是拿來形容早晨太陽升起，然後發光照耀大地的樣子，後來引申作「醒來；起床」解 (= *wake up*)。所以這句話的意思是「我醒來以後，會伸個懶腰。」也可以說成：When I get up, I stretch my arms and legs. (當我起床之後，我會伸展一下手腳。)

　　　【arm〔ɑrm〕*n.* 手臂　　leg〔lɛg〕*n.* 腿；腳】

5

rise and shine 是美國人常講的話，其用法舉例
如下：

I *rise and shine* at 6:30. (我六點半起床。)

Come on, children! *Rise and shine!*
　We're going to the beach.
(來吧，孩子們！起床囉！我們要去海邊了。)

Father always yells, "*Rise and shine!*" in the
　morning when we want to go on sleeping.
(當我們早上想要繼續睡時，爸爸總是會大喊：
　「起床囉！」)

5

come on 來吧；好啦
children 〔'tʃɪldrən〕 *n. pl.* 孩子們
beach 〔 bitʃ 〕 *n.* 海邊
yell 〔 jɛl 〕 *v.* 大喊　　*go on* 繼續

6. *I eat at home or on the way.*
on the way 在途中

　　這句話是由 I either eat at home or eat on the
way to school. 省略而來，意思是「我會在家裡吃，
或是在上學的途中吃。」on the way 這個片語是作
「在途中」解，如果要說明是在去某個地方的途中，
介系詞要用 to，例如：I met Kelly *on the way to*
the park. (我在去公園的途中遇到凱莉。)

either…or~ 不是…就是~；…或~
meet 〔 mit 〕 *v.* 遇見

7. ***I hit the books again there.***

hit the books 用功唸書　　again〔ə'gεn〕*adv.* 再一次

　　　hit 的主要意思就是「打」，而 hit the books 字面上的意思就是「打書」，也就是我們常說的「K書；用功唸書」。所以，這句話的意思就是「我在那裡再用功唸一次書。」也可以說成：

I study very hard there.
（我在那裡非常用功唸書。）

I study some more there.
（我在那裡會多唸一點書。）

【hard〔hɑrd〕*adv.* 努力地】

5

8. ***I relax and take a break.***

relax〔rɪ'læks〕*v.* 放鬆　　break〔brek〕*n.* 休息時間
take a break 休息一下（= *take a rest*）

　　　這句話的意思是「我會放輕鬆，然後休息一下。」break 在這裡當名詞用，作「休息時間」解，所以 take a break 就是「休息一下」的意思。

　　　中國人常說「休息是爲了走更長遠的路。」在英文裡面，有很多不同的說法，我們依照使用頻率排列：

① ***Take a break.***【第一常用】

② Take a rest.（休息一下。）【第二常用】
　　【rest〔rεst〕*n.* 休息】

③ Take it easy.（放輕鬆。）【第三常用】

④ Take five.（休息一下；休息五分鐘。）

9. *I sleep late and have a ball.*

sleep〔slip〕*v.* 睡　　late〔let〕*adv.* 晚
have a ball 玩得痛快

　　這句話的意思是「我會睡到很晚，而且玩得很痛快。」ball 這個字的主要意思是「球」，但也可以作「舞會」解，對老外來說，參加舞會通常都會玩得很開心，所以後來 have a ball 就引申為「玩得痛快」(= *have fun* = *have a good time*)。這句話還可以說成：I get up late and have fun. (我很晚才起床，而且玩得很痛快。)

5

10. *Is your day the same as mine?*

same〔sem〕*adj.* 相同的　　*the same as* 和～相同
mine〔maɪn〕*pron.* 我的 (東西)

　　這句話字面的意思是「你的日子也跟我的一樣嗎？」引申為「你也過著和我一樣的日子嗎？」也可以說成：Does my day sound like your day? (我的日子聽起來跟你的日子一樣嗎？)【sound〔saʊnd〕*v.* 聽起來】

the same as「和～相同」的用法舉例如下：

My bag is *the same as* yours.
(我的袋子跟你的一樣。)

The student made *the same* mistake *as* last time. (那個學生犯了和上次相同的錯誤。)

bag〔bæg〕*n.* 袋子　　student〔'stjudn̩t〕*n.* 學生
mistake〔mə'stek〕*n.* 錯誤　　*last time* 上一次

My Daily Schedule

Everybody has a daily schedule. We do the same things almost every day. My typical day is probably like yours.

Here's my daily routine. I get up at 6:30 every morning. I take my time waking up, but then I wash up quickly. I brush my teeth, comb my hair and put on my school uniform. I pack my bag for school and I leave. I never miss breakfast, so I either eat at home or eat on the way to school. But I always eat in a hurry. After school, I go to a cram school like all my friends. I study and finish my homework for the day. *Finally*, I go home and I take a break. I have dinner with my family, watch a little TV and just relax. I am usually in bed by 9:30.

This is my routine from Monday to Friday. *However*, the weekends are different. I can wake up late and have a ball. *Then*, I can do whatever I like. I believe my routine is typical. It is probably a lot like yours.

5

● 中文翻譯

我的日常作息

　　每個人都有日常作息時間表。我們幾乎每天都做一樣的事。我可能跟你過著同樣平凡的日子。

　　以下就是我每天都做的事。我每天早上六點半起床。我從容地起床，然後很快地洗把臉。我會刷牙、梳頭髮，還有穿上學校的制服。我會把上學要用的東西裝進袋子裡，然後就出門。我從來不會不吃早餐，所以我不是在家裡吃，就是在上學的途中吃。但是我總是吃得很急。放學後，我就像我所有的朋友一樣，會到補習班去。我會唸書，然後完成當天的家庭作業。最後，我會回到家休息。我會和家人一起吃晚餐，然後看一下電視來放鬆一下。我通常九點半以前會上床睡覺。

　　這就是我從星期一到星期五的例行公事。但是，週末就不一樣了。我可以睡到很晚，而且玩得很痛快。然後我可以做任何我想做的事。我認為我每天做的事都很平凡。我過的日子可能很像你們的。

6. My School Life

I love school.
I think school is really cool.
Let me tell you about my school life.

I go to school five days a week.
I'm there eight hours each day.
School is a big part of my life.

My school day is long.
My schedule is so full.
There is always something going on.

6

life〔laɪf〕   really〔'rɪəlɪ〕
cool〔kul〕   let〔lɛt〕
week〔wik〕   there〔ðɛr〕
hour〔aʊr〕   each〔itʃ〕
part〔pɑrt〕   schedule〔'skɛdʒʊl〕
full〔fʊl〕   always〔'ɔlwez〕
something〔'sʌmθɪŋ〕   *go on*

6

My teachers are excellent.

They help me to improve.

They are very patient and kind.

My classmates are good friends.

We often study together.

We always help each other out.

We are like a team.

We play games and enjoy activities.

We laugh and have fun when we can.

---

excellent〔'ɛkslənt〕　　　improve〔ɪm'pruv〕

patient〔'peʃənt〕　　　　kind〔kaɪnd〕

classmate〔'klæs‚met〕

often〔'ɔfən〕　　　　　　study〔'stʌdɪ〕

together〔tə'gɛðɚ〕　　　*help sb. out*

each other　　　　　　like〔laɪk〕

team〔tim〕　　　　　　　activity〔æk'tɪvətɪ〕

laugh〔læf〕　　　　　　　fun〔fʌn〕

My schoolwork keeps me busy.

I have homework every day.

I have quizzes and tests all the time.

I like learning new things.

I know knowledge is power.

I'm preparing for the future.

My school is like a family.

It's like a home away from home.

I hope you feel the same way about

　your school.

6

---

schoolwork ('skul,wɜk)

keep (kip)   busy ('bɪzɪ)

homework ('hom,wɜk)   quiz (kwɪz)

test (tɛst)   *all the time*

learn (lɜn)   knowledge ('nɑlɪdʒ)

power ('pauɚ)   prepare (prɪ'pɛr)

future ('fjutʃɚ)   hope (hop)

same (sem)   *the same way*

6. My School Life

◯ 演講解說

I love school.
I think school is really cool.
Let me tell you about my
   school life.

I go to school five days a week.
I'm there eight hours each day.
School is a big part of my life.

My school day is long.
My schedule is so full.
There is always something
   going on.

我愛學校。
我覺得學校真的很棒。
讓我把我的學校生活講給你
們聽。

我一星期有五天要上學。
我每天在那裡待八小時。
學校佔了我生活的一大部分。

我的上課時間很長。
我的課程表很滿。
總是有事在發生；總是有活
動在進行。

** ————————————————

life〔laɪf〕*n.* 生活；人生　　really〔'rɪəlɪ〕*adv.* 非常；很
cool〔kul〕*adj.* 很棒的　　let〔lɛt〕*v.* 讓　　*go to school* 上學
hour〔aʊr〕*n.* 小時　　each〔itʃ〕*adj.* 每個的
school day 上課時間　　schedule〔'skɛdʒʊl〕*n.* 時間表；課程表
full〔fʊl〕*adj.* 滿的　　always〔'ɔlwez〕*adv.* 總是
something〔'sʌmθɪŋ〕*pron.* 某事　　*go on* 發生；進行

My teachers are excellent.	我的老師很優秀。
They help me to improve.	他們幫助我進步。
They are very patient and kind.	他們很有耐心，而且很親切。
My classmates are good friends.	同學都是我的好朋友。
We often study together.	我們常常一起唸書。
We always help each other out.	我們總是互相幫忙。
We are like a team.	我們就像是一個團隊。
We play games and enjoy activities.	我們玩遊戲，而且喜歡做活動。
We laugh and have fun when we can.	我們一有機會就會笑和玩樂。

6

** ————————————

excellent〔ˈɛksḷənt〕*adj.* 優秀的　　improve〔ɪmˈpruv〕*v.* 進步

patient〔ˈpeʃənt〕*adj.* 有耐心的　　kind〔kaɪnd〕*adj.* 親切的

classmate〔ˈklæsˌmet〕*n.* 同學　　often〔ˈɔfən〕*adv.* 常常

study〔ˈstʌdɪ〕*v.* 讀書　　together〔təˈɡɛðɚ〕*adv.* 一起

help sb. out 幫忙某人　　*each other* 彼此；互相

like〔laɪk〕*prep.* 像　　team〔tim〕*n.* 隊；組

enjoy〔ɪnˈdʒɔɪ〕*v.* 喜歡　　activity〔ækˈtɪvətɪ〕*n.* 活動

laugh〔læf〕*v.* 笑　　fun〔fʌn〕*n.* 樂趣

have fun 玩樂；玩得愉快

My schoolwork keeps me busy.	我的課業使我忙碌。
I have homework every day.	我每天都有家庭作業。
I have quizzes and tests all the time.	我經常有小考和測驗。
I like learning new things.	我喜歡學習新事物。
I know knowledge is power.	我了解知識就是力量。
I'm preparing for the future.	我正在替未來作準備。
My school is like a family.	我的學校就像是一個家庭。
It's like a home away from home.	它就像是另一個家。
I hope you feel the same way about your school.	我希望你對你的學校也有相同的感受。

6

** ——————————————

schoolwork〔'skul,wɜk〕 *n.* 功課；學業
keep〔kip〕 *v.* 使維持（某種狀態）　　busy〔'bɪzɪ〕 *adj.* 忙碌的
homework〔'hom,wɜk〕 *n.* 家庭作業　　quiz〔kwɪz〕 *n.* 小考
test〔tɛst〕 *n.* 測驗　　*all the time* 經常；總是
learn〔lɜn〕 *v.* 學習　　knowledge〔'nɑlɪdʒ〕 *n.* 知識
power〔'pauɚ〕 *n.* 力量　　prepare〔prɪ'pɛr〕 *v.* 準備
future〔'fjutʃɚ〕 *n.* 未來　　*away from* 遠離
hope〔hop〕 *v.* 希望　　same〔sem〕 *adj.* 相同的
the same way 同樣地

背景說明

　　小朋友每天都要上學，上學非常有趣，老師會教我們很多東西，同學會陪我們一起聊天玩耍，雖然有時候要考試，但是上學還是一件很開心的事。本篇演講稿，就是要教你用英文介紹多采多姿的校園生活。

1. ***I go to school five days a week.***

   go to school 上學　　week〔wik〕*n.* 星期

　　　　這句話的意思是「我一星期有五天要上學。」也可以說成：I attend school from Monday to Friday.

　　（我從星期一到星期五都要上學。）

　　【attend〔ə'tɛnd〕*v.* 上（學）】

　　　　當你要說明自己多久做一次某件事時，類似的說法還有很多，舉例如下：

　　　　I exercise three times a week.

　　　　（我一星期運動三次。）

　　　　We visit our grandparents two times
　　　　　a month.

　　　　（我們一個月去探望祖父母兩次。）

　　　　exercise〔'ɛksɚˌsaɪz〕*v.* 運動
　　　　time〔taɪm〕*n.* 次　　visit〔'vɪzɪt〕*v.* 拜訪；探望
　　　　grandparents〔'grændˌpɛrənts〕*n. pl.* 祖父母
　　　　month〔mʌnθ〕*n.* 月

2. **I'm there eight hours each day.**

there〔ðɛr〕*adv.* 在那裡　　hour〔aʊr〕*n.* 小時
each〔itʃ〕*adj.* 每個的

　　這句話的意思是「我每天在那裡待八小時。」也可以說成：I'm there eight hours *a* day.（我一天在那裡待八小時。）

3. **There is always something going on.**

always〔'ɔlwez〕*adv.* 總是
something〔'sʌmθɪŋ〕*pron.* 某事
go on 發生；進行

6

　　go on 這個片語作「發生」解，例如美國人打招呼時會說：Hey! What's *going on*?（嘿！發生什麼事？）當他們說這句話時，其實不是真的在問你最近發生什麼事，而只是單純的問好而已。所以這句話的意思是「總是有事在發生；總是有活動在進行。」也可以說成：

We're always doing something.
（我們總是在做某件事。）
We are never idle!（我們從來不會閒著！）
Our schedule is always full.
（我們的課程表總是滿滿的。）

idle〔'aɪdl̩〕*adj.* 閒著的
schedule〔'skɛdʒʊl〕*n.* 時間表；課程表
full〔fʊl〕*adj.* 滿滿的

4. ***They help me to improve.***

improve〔ɪm'pruv〕v. 改進；進步

　　　　這句話的意思是「他們幫助我進步。」help 這個
動詞很特別，它後面可以接原形動詞，或是不定詞。

【比較】***I helped him look for his key.***【正】
　　　　（我幫他找鑰匙。）

　　　　I helped him to look for his key.【正】

　　　　I helped him looking for his key.【誤】

5. ***We always help each other out.***

help sb. out 幫忙某人　　***each other*** 彼此；互相

　　　　很多人弄不清楚 ***help sb. out*** 和 help sb. 的區
別，兩者意義相同，只是 ***help sb. out*** 比 help sb.
的語氣緩和。【詳見「一口氣英語②」p.4-6】

【比較】　Please help me.【語氣嚴肅】
　　　　（請幫助我；請救救我。）

　　　　Please help me out.【語氣輕鬆】
　　　　（請你幫幫我的忙。）

　　　　We always help each other out. 的意思是「我
們總是互相幫忙。」如果說成：We always help each
other. 意思就是「我們總是互相幫助。」這兩句話意思
相同，只是語氣不同。

6

6. ***We are like a team***.

like〔laɪk〕*prep.* 像　　team〔tim〕*n.* 隊;組

　　　這句話的意思是「我們就像是一個團隊。」like
主要是當動詞用,作「喜歡」解,例如:I *like* this
book.(我喜歡這本書。)但在這裡
是當介系詞用,作「像」解,例如:

We're *like* a family.
(我們就像是一家人。)

Everyone says I look just *like* my mother.
(大家都說我長得很像我媽。)

7. ***We laugh and have fun when we can***.

laugh〔læf〕*v.* 笑　　fun〔fʌn〕*n.* 樂趣
have fun 玩樂;玩得愉快

　　　這句話字面的意思是「當我們可以時,我們會笑和
玩樂。」引申爲「我們一有機會就會笑和玩樂。」have
fun 是作「玩樂;玩得愉快」解,等於 enjoy *oneself*
和 have a good time。所以,這句話也可以說成:

When we get the chance, we enjoy ourselves.
(我們一有機會,就會玩得很愉快。)

We have a good time whenever we are free.
(我們一有空,就會玩得很開心。)

get〔gɛt〕*v.* 獲得　　chance〔tʃæns〕*n.* 機會
whenever〔hwɛn'ɛvɚ〕*conj.* 無論何時;每當
free〔fri〕*adj.* 有空閒的

8. ***My schoolwork keeps me busy.***

schoolwork〔'skul͵wɝk〕*n.* 功課；學業

keep〔kip〕*v.* 使維持（某種狀態）

busy〔'bɪzɪ〕*adj.* 忙碌的

　　這句話的意思是「我的課業使我忙碌。」keep 這個字作「使維持（某種狀態）」解時，須用「keep ＋ 受詞 ＋ 受詞補語」的形式，來使句意完整，例如：

This coat will ***keep*** you <u>warm</u>.
受詞補語

（這件外套可以讓你暖和。）

The noise ***kept*** her <u>awake</u>.
受詞補語

（噪音使她一直醒著。）

coat〔kot〕*n.* 外套　　warm〔wɔrm〕*adj.* 溫暖的

noise〔nɔɪz〕*n.* 噪音　　awake〔ə'wek〕*adj.* 醒著的

9. ***I have quizzes and tests all the time.***

quiz〔kwɪz〕*n.* 小考　　test〔tɛst〕*n.* 測驗

all the time 經常；總是

　　這句話的意思是「我經常有小考和測驗。」all the time 在此作「經常」解（＝ *frequently*），例如：

My best friend and I are together ***all the time***.

（我的好朋友和我經常在一起。）

It's sunny ***all the time*** in Hawaii.

（夏威夷經常都是晴天。）

frequently〔'frikwəntlɪ〕*adv.* 經常

together〔tə'gɛðɚ〕*adv.* 一起　　sunny〔'sʌnɪ〕*adj.* 晴朗的

Hawaii〔hə'waɪi〕*n.* 夏威夷

10. ***It's like a home away from home.***
    away from 遠離

　　　　這句話的字面意思是「它就像是家之外的家。」引申爲「它就像是另一個家。」就是說，待在學校，感覺就像待在家裡一樣舒服自在。這句話還可以說成：

It's like my second home.
（它就像是我的第二個家。）

I feel very comfortable there.
（我在那裡覺得很舒服。）

It feels like I'm home when I'm there.
（我在那裡時，感覺就像在家裡一樣。）

second〔'sɛkənd〕*adj.* 第二的　　feel〔fil〕*v.* 覺得
comfortable〔'kʌmfɚtəb!〕*adj.* 舒服的

6

11. ***I hope you feel the same way about your school.***
    hope〔hop〕*v.* 希望　　same〔sem〕*adj.* 相同的
    the same way 同樣地

　　　　這句話的意思是「我希望你對你的學校也有相同的感受。」feel the same way 的意思是「有同樣的感覺；有相同的感受」。也可以說成：I hope you have similar feelings about your school. （我希望你對你的學校也有相同的感受。）

similar〔'sɪmələ〕*adj.* 類似的；相同的
feeling〔'filɪŋ〕*n.* 感受

作文範例

My School Life

We are all students right now. School is a very important part of our lives because we can learn many things in school.

I love school and here are my reasons why. For one thing, my teachers are excellent. They always help me to improve. I'm so lucky, because they are very patient and kind. Another reason is my classmates and I are good friends. We always help each other when we study together. We are like a team. When we play games and enjoy activities, we always have so much fun.

My schoolwork keeps me busy because I have homework every day. I have quizzes and tests all the time. But I like learning new things because I'm preparing for the future. My school is like my second home. I always feel comfortable and welcome in school. Many students feel the same way about school as I do.

6

● 中文翻譯

我的學校生活

我們現在都是學生。學校對我們的生活來說,是非常重要的一部份,因為我們可以在學校裡學到很多東西。

我愛學校,而以下就是我愛學校的理由。首先,我的老師很優秀。他們總是幫助我進步。我很幸運,因為他們都很有耐心又很親切。另一個原因是,同學和我都是好朋友。我們一起唸書時,總是會互相幫助。我們就像是一個團隊。當我們玩遊戲和做活動時,總是玩得很開心。

我的課業使我忙碌,因為我每天都有家庭作業。我經常有小考和測驗。但是我喜歡學習新事物,因為我要替未來做準備。我的學校就像是我的第二個家。我在學校總是覺得自在而且受歡迎。許多學生對於學校的感受都跟我一樣。

7. My Favorite Teacher

I have a favorite teacher.
Her name is Miss Lee.
She is so wonderful to me.

She has a sweet personality.
She's very patient and kind.
She never gets angry or yells.

She encourages me.
She compliments my efforts.
She makes me feel special all the time.

7

favorite (ˈfevərɪt)	Miss (mɪs)
wonderful (ˈwʌndəfəl)	sweet (swit)
personality (ˌpɝsṇˈælətɪ)	patient (ˈpeʃənt)
kind (kaɪnd)	angry (ˈæŋgrɪ)
yell (jɛl)	encourage (ɪnˈkɝɪdʒ)
compliment (ˈkɑmpləˌmɛnt)	
effort (ˈɛfɚt)	special (ˈspɛʃəl)
all the time	

Her class is interesting.

We do many different things.

We never feel tired or bored.

She's charming and bright.

She's an expert for sure.

She answers every question we ask.

She demands a lot.

She gives lots of homework.

But we always work hard to

    please her.

7

---

class (klæs)

different ('dɪfərənt)

bored (bord)

bright (braɪt)

for sure

question ('kwɛstʃən)

demand (dɪ'mænd)

please (pliz)

interesting ('ɪntrɪstɪŋ)

tired (taɪrd)

charming ('tʃɑrmɪŋ)

expert ('ɛkspɝt)

answer ('ænsɚ)

ask (æsk)

homework ('hom,wɝk)

The little things make her great.

Her smile warms my heart.

Her simple praise is music to my
ears.

She's a good listener.

She's very understanding.

She's fair to everyone.

She brightens up my day.

I'll never forget her.

I'll remember her forever.

7

little ('lɪtḷ)   great (gret)

smile (smaɪl)   warm (wɔrm)

heart (hɑrt)   simple ('sɪmpḷ)

praise (prez)   music ('mjuzɪk)

be music to one's ears   listener ('lɪsṇə˞)

understanding (ˌʌndə˞'stændɪŋ)

fair (fɛr)   brighten ('braɪtṇ)

forget (fə˞'gɛt)   remember (rɪ'mɛmbə˞)

forever (fə˞'ɛvə˞)

7. My Favorite Teacher

● 演講解說

I have a favorite teacher.	我最喜歡一位老師。
Her name is Miss Lee.	她的名字是李小姐。
She is so wonderful to me.	她對我非常好。
She has a sweet personality.	她的個性溫柔。
She's very patient and kind.	她非常有耐心，而且又親切。
She never gets angry or yells.	她從來不會生氣或大叫。
She encourages me.	她會鼓勵我。
She compliments my efforts.	她會誇獎我的努力。
She makes me feel special all the time.	她總是讓我覺得自己很特別。

7

＊＊ ──────────────

favorite〔'fevərɪt〕adj. 最喜歡的　　name〔nem〕n. 名字
Miss〔mɪs〕n. 小姐　　wonderful〔'wʌndəfəl〕adj. 很棒的
sweet〔swit〕adj. 溫柔的　　personality〔͵pɝsn'ælətɪ〕n. 個性
patient〔'peʃənt〕adj. 有耐心的　　kind〔kaɪnd〕adj. 親切的
get〔gɛt〕v. 變得　　angry〔'æŋgrɪ〕adj. 生氣的
yell〔jɛl〕v. 大叫　　encourage〔ɪn'kɝɪdʒ〕v. 鼓勵
compliment〔'kɑmplə͵mɛnt〕v. 稱讚；誇獎　　effort〔'ɛfət〕n. 努力
special〔'spɛʃəl〕adj. 特別的　　*all the time* 經常；總是

Her class is interesting.

We do many different things.

We never feel tired or bored.

她的課很有趣。

我們會做許多不同的事。

我們從來不會覺得累或無聊。

She's charming and bright.

She's an expert for sure.

She answers every question
　we ask.

她既迷人又開朗。

她一定是個專家。

她會回答我們問的每一個
問題。

She demands a lot.

She gives lots of homework.

But we always work hard to
　please her.

她的要求很多。

她會出很多家庭作業。

但是我們總是會努力用功來
取悅她。

7

** ——————————

class〔klæs〕*n.* 課程　　interesting〔'ɪntrɪstɪŋ〕*adj.* 有趣的

different〔'dɪfərənt〕*adj.* 不同的

tired〔taɪrd〕*adj.* 疲倦的；累的　　bored〔bord〕*adj.* 無聊的

charming〔'tʃɑrmɪŋ〕*adj.* 迷人的

bright〔braɪt〕*adj.* 開朗的；聰明的

expert〔'ɛkspɝt〕*n.* 專家　　*for sure* 一定

answer〔'ænsɚ〕*v.* 回答　　question〔'kwɛstʃən〕*n.* 問題

ask〔æsk〕*v.* 問　　demand〔dɪ'mænd〕*v.* 要求

homework〔'hom,wɝk〕*n.* 家庭作業　　*work hard* 努力用功

please〔pliz〕*v.* 使高興；取悅

The little things make her great.	一些小事使她變得了不起。
Her smile warms my heart.	她的微笑溫暖我的心。
Her simple praise is music to my ears.	她簡單的讚美非常悅耳。
She's a good listener.	她是個好聽眾。
She's very understanding.	她非常體貼。
She's fair to everyone.	她公平對待每個人。
She brightens up my day.	她使我的日子過得很快樂。
I'll never forget her.	我絕不會忘記她。
I'll remember her forever.	我會永遠記得她。

7

** ————————————————————————

little〔'lɪtḷ〕*adj.* 小的;微不足道的　　make〔mek〕*v.* 使…成為

great〔gret〕*adj.* 優秀的;偉大的　　smile〔smaɪl〕*n.* 微笑

warm〔wɔrm〕*v.* 使溫暖　　heart〔hɑrt〕*n.* 心

simple〔'sɪmpḷ〕*adj.* 簡單的　　praise〔prez〕*n.* 讚美

music〔'mjuzɪk〕*n.* 音樂　　ear〔ɪr〕*n.* 耳朵

be music to one's ***ears*** 令某人感覺悅耳

listener〔'lɪsnɚ〕*n.* 傾聽者;聽眾

understanding〔ˌʌndɚ'stændɪŋ〕*adj.* 體貼的;體諒的

fair〔fɛr〕*adj.* 公平的　　brighten〔'braɪtn̩〕*v.* 使愉快 < *up* >

forget〔fɚ'gɛt〕*v.* 忘記　　remember〔rɪ'mɛmbɚ〕*v.* 記得

forever〔fɚ'ɛvɚ〕*adv.* 永遠

●背景說明

　　俗話說:「一日爲師,終身爲父。」一位好老師,不但會爲你解答課業上的問題,還會指引你正確的人生方向,幫助你邁向成功。本篇演講稿句句優美如詩,教你用最美的語言,來介紹自己最喜歡的老師。

1. *Her name is Miss Lee.*

   Miss〔mɪs〕 *n.* 小姐

   　　這句話的意思是「她的名字是李小姐。」中國人稱「李老師」,但是外國人不説:*Teacher Lee*(誤)。他們稱呼男老師,是用 Mr.〔ˈmɪstɚ〕,例如 Mr. Liu(劉老師);而稱呼女老師,未婚用 Miss,已婚用 Mrs.〔ˈmɪsɪz〕;  如果不確定這位女老師結婚了沒,就可以用 Ms.〔mɪz〕。

2. *She is so wonderful to me.*

   wonderful〔ˈwʌndɚfəl〕 *adj.* 很棒的

   　　wonderful 是美國人很常用的形容詞,它可以作「很棒的;很好的」(= *great*) 解。所以這句話的意思是「她對我非常好。」也可以説成:She treats me great.(她對我很好。)

   treat〔trit〕 *v.* 對待　　great〔gret〕 *adv.* 很好 (= *very well*)

3. **She never gets angry or yells.**

get〔gɛt〕v. 變得　　angry〔'æŋgrɪ〕adj. 生氣的
yell〔jɛl〕v. 大叫

　　這句話的意思是「她從來不會生氣或大叫。」get
的主要意思是「得到」，例如：I **got** this book from
my dad. (我從我爸那邊得到這本書。) 但在這裡，
get 是作「變得」(= become) 解，其用法舉例如下：

My dad **got** very fat after he quit smoking.
(我爸戒菸之後變得很胖。)

The weather **gets** cold every winter.
(每年冬天天氣都會變得很冷。)

After 10 p.m., I **get** very sleepy.
(晚上十點之後，我變得很想睡。)

dad〔dæd〕n. 爸爸　　fat〔fæt〕adj. 肥胖的
quit〔kwɪt〕v. 停止　　smoking〔'smokɪŋ〕n. 吸煙
weather〔'wɛðɚ〕n. 天氣　　winter〔'wɪntɚ〕n. 冬天
p.m. 下午　　sleepy〔'slipɪ〕adj. 想睡的

4. **She makes me feel special all the time.**

feel〔fil〕v. 覺得　　special〔'spɛʃəl〕adj. 特別的
all the time 經常；總是

　　這句話是由 She makes me feel that I am so
special all the time. 省略而來，意思是「她總是讓我
覺得自己很特別。」也可以說成：She always makes
me feel wonderful. (她總是讓我覺得自己很棒。)

5. *She's an expert for sure*.

　　expert〔'ɛkspɝt〕*n.* 專家　　*for sure* 一定

　　　　這句話的意思是「她一定是個專家。」*for sure*
　　是作「一定；確實地（ = *definitely*) 解，例如：

　　　　I'll be there before dinner *for sure*.
　　　　（我一定會在晚餐之前到達那裡。）

　　　　He said he could do it *for sure*.
　　　　（他說他一定辦得到。）

　　　　Please give it to me; I can fix it *for sure*.
　　　　（請把它交給我，我一定可以修好它。）

　　　　I promise, we'll win *for sure*.
　　　　（我保證，我們一定會贏。）

　　　　before〔bɪ'for〕*prep.* 在…之前
　　　　dinner〔'dɪnɚ〕*n.* 晚餐　　fix〔fɪks〕*v.* 修理
　　　　promise〔'prɑmɪs〕*v.* 保證　　win〔wɪn〕*v.* 贏

7

6. *She demands a lot*.

　　demand〔dɪ'mænd〕*v.* 要求
　　a lot 很多

　　　　這句話的意思是「她的要求
　　很多。」demand 在這裡是當動詞用，作「要求」
　　（ = *require*) 解。這句話還可以說成：

　　　　She requests a lot. (她的要求很多。)
　　　　She asks for a lot. (她的要求很多。)

　　　　【request〔rɪ'kwɛst〕*v.* 要求　　*ask for* 要求】

7. *But we always work hard to please her.*

work hard 努力用功　　please〔pliz〕*v.* 使高興；取悅

　　這句話的意思是「但是我們總是會努力用功來取悅她。」please 的主要意思是「請」，但在這裡是作「使高興；取悅」解。這句話也可以說成：

We try hard to make her happy.
（我們會努力使她高興。）

We work diligently to satisfy her.
（我們會努力用功來使她滿意。）

hard〔hɑrd〕*adv.* 努力地　　make〔mek〕*v.* 使
diligently〔'dɪlədʒəntlɪ〕*adv.* 勤勉地
satisfy〔'sætɪs‚faɪ〕*v.* 使滿意

7

8. *The little things make her great.*

little〔'lɪtl̩〕*adj.* 小的；微不足道的
make〔mek〕*v.* 使　　great〔gret〕*adj.* 優秀的；偉大的

　　這句話的意思是「一些小事使她變得了不起。」the little things 指的是生活中的一些小事，舉例來說，優秀的老師，除了傳授專業知識給學生之外，還會注意到學生穿得夠不夠多，有沒有吃早餐等等，而這些小事，都會讓學生更加喜歡老師。

　　這句話也可以說成：Her small acts of kindness are why she's so wonderful.（她親切的小動作就是她如此了不起的原因。）【kindness〔'kaɪndnɪs〕*n.* 親切；體貼】

9. *Her smile warms my heart.*

smile〔smaɪl〕*n.* 微笑　　warm〔wɔrm〕*v.* 使溫暖
heart〔hɑrt〕*n.* 心

　　這句話的意思是「她的微笑溫暖我的心。」這是一句非常優美的話，一定要背下來，除了在介紹你最喜歡的老師時，可以派上用場之外，平常也可以對朋友說：Your smile warms my heart. 保證他們會笑得更燦爛。這句話還可以說成：

Her smile is like a beautiful sunset.
（她的微笑就像是美麗的落日。）

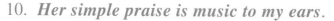

Her smile melts my heart.
（她的微笑融化我的心。）

She smiles like a beautiful angel.
（她笑得像個美麗的天使。）

beautiful〔'bjutəfəl〕*adj.* 美麗的
sunset〔'sʌn,sɛt〕*n.* 落日　　melt〔mɛlt〕*v.* 融化
angel〔'endʒəl〕*n.* 天使

7

10. *Her simple praise is music to my ears.*

simple〔'sɪmpḷ〕*adj.* 簡單的　　praise〔prez〕*n.* 讚美
music〔'mjuzɪk〕*n.* 音樂　　ear〔ɪr〕*n.* 耳朵
be music to** one's **ears 令某人感覺悅耳

　　這句話是由 Her simple praise is like music to my ears. 省略而來，字面的意思是「她簡單的讚美對我的耳朵來說，就像音樂一樣。」引申為「她簡單的讚美非常悅耳。」

這句話也可以說成：

> I love to hear her praise. (我愛聽她的讚美。)
>
> Her praise sounds wonderful to me.
> (對我來說，她的讚美聽起來很棒。)
>
> A compliment from her means a lot to me.
> (她的讚美對我來說意義重大。)

hear〔hɪr〕v. 聽到　　sound〔saʊnd〕v. 聽起來
wonderful〔'wʌndəfəl〕adj. 很棒的
compliment〔'kɑmpləmənt〕n. 稱讚
mean〔min〕v. 有⋯的意義

11. ***She brightens up my day.***

brighten〔'braɪtn̩〕v. 使愉快 < *up* >

brighten up 原本的意思是「使明亮」，但在這裡引申作「使愉快」(= *cheer up*) 解。所以，這句話的意思是「她使我的日子過得很快樂。」也可以說成：

> She cheers me up. (她使我高興。)
> She makes me happy. (她使我開心。)
>
> She adds joy to my day.
> (她為我的日子增添歡樂。)
> She is like a ray of sunshine.
> (她就像是一道陽光。)

cheer〔tʃɪr〕v. 使高興　　add〔æd〕v. 增加
joy〔dʒɔɪ〕n. 歡樂　　ray〔re〕n. 光線
sunshine〔'sʌn,ʃaɪn〕n. 陽光

7

○ 作文範例

My Favorite Teacher

When students attend school, teachers become the most important people to them. That is because teachers are responsible for training students and guiding them. I would like to tell you about my favorite teacher. Her name is Miss Lee.

Miss Lee has a great personality. She's very patient and kind. She never gets angry or yells; she always encourages me instead. She compliments me on my efforts and makes me feel special all the time. She's a very good listener and quite understanding. Most important of all, Miss Lee is fair to everyone.

Her class is interesting because we do many different things. We never feel bored or tired. Miss Lee is charming and bright, and she answers every question we ask. But she demands a lot, too. She gives lots of homework, but we always work hard to please her.

I love going to school because of Miss Lee. I'll never forget her. I am grateful to her for making school so interesting and so much fun. I'll remember her forever.

7

● 中文翻譯

我最喜歡的老師

　　當學生們去上學時，老師對他們來說，就成為最重要的人。那是因為老師要負責訓練和指導學生。我想要告訴你們我最喜歡的老師。她的名字是李小姐。

　　李小姐的個性很好。她很有耐心又親切。她從來不會生氣或大叫；相反地，她總是鼓勵我。她會誇獎我的努力，總是讓我覺得自己很特別。她是個很棒的聽眾，而且很體貼。最重要的是，李小姐會公平對待每個人。

　　她的課很有趣，因為我們會做許多不同的事。我們從來不會覺得無聊或累。李小姐既迷人又開朗，而且她會回答我們問的每個問題。但是她的要求也很多。她會出很多家庭作業，可是我們總是會努力用功來取悅她。

　　因為李小姐的關係，所以我喜歡上學。我絕不會忘記她。我很感謝她，因為她把學校變得非常有趣、非常好玩。我會永遠記得她。

8. My Favorite Places

I like many places.
I enjoy many spots.
Here are three of my favorites.

I'll start with the zoo.
The animals are amazing.
Some are cute and some are ugly.

Some are very strange.
I like to pet and feed them.
I enjoy seeing them perform.

8

favorite (ˈfevərɪt)	place (ples)
spot (spat)	start (start)
zoo (zu)	animal (ˈænəmļ)
amazing (əˈmezɪŋ)	cute (kjut)
ugly (ˈʌglɪ)	strange (strendʒ)
pet (pɛt)	feed (fid)
enjoy (ɪnˈdʒɔɪ)	perform (pəˈfɔrm)

Museums are cool, too.

The exhibits are terrific.

The displays are fascinating.

I like famous things.

I enjoy works of art.

Maybe someday my work will be there.

History tells me about the past.

Science shows me the future.

From dinosaurs to robots, I love it all.

museum〔 mju'ziəm 〕

exhibit〔 ɪg'zɪbɪt 〕

display〔 dɪ'sple 〕

famous〔'feməs 〕

art〔 ɑrt 〕

someday〔'sʌm,de 〕

past〔 pæst 〕

show〔 ʃo 〕

dinosaur〔'daɪnə,sɔr 〕

love〔 lʌv 〕

cool〔 kul 〕

terrific〔 tə'rɪfɪk 〕

fascinating〔'fæsṇ,etɪŋ 〕

work〔 wɝk 〕

maybe〔'mebɪ 〕

history〔'hɪstrɪ 〕

science〔'saɪəns 〕

future〔'fjutʃɚ 〕

robot〔'robət 〕

8

Finally, amusement parks are a blast.
I'm crazy about wild rides.
Roller coasters are the best.

It's fun to scream.
It's fun to be scared.
I don't care if I get dizzy

Hey, I'm curious about you.
Where do you like to go?
What's your favorite place?

---

finally ('faɪnḷɪ)

amusement (ə'mjuzmənt)

amusement park

blast (blæst)

crazy ('krezɪ)

wild (waɪld)

ride (raɪd)

roller coaster

best (bɛst)

fun (fʌn)

scream (skrim)

scared (skɛrd)

care (kɛr)

dizzy ('dɪzɪ)

hey (he)

curious ('kjʊrɪəs)

8

8. My Favorite Places

🔵 演講解說

I like many places.	我喜歡很多地方。
I enjoy many spots.	我喜歡很多場所。
Here are three of my favorites.	以下是我最喜歡的三個地方。
I'll start with the zoo.	我將從動物園開始說。
The animals are amazing.	那些動物真是不可思議。
Some are cute and some are ugly.	牠們有些很可愛，有些很醜。
Some are very strange.	有些動物非常奇怪。
I like to pet and feed them.	我喜歡摸牠們，還有餵牠們吃東西。
I enjoy seeing them perform.	我喜歡看牠們表演。

** ——————————————————————————

favorite〔'fevərɪt〕*adj.* 最喜歡的　*n.* 最喜歡的人、事、物
spot〔spɑt〕*n.* 地點　　start〔stɑrt〕*v.* 開始　　zoo〔zu〕*n.* 動物園
amazing〔ə'mezɪŋ〕*adj.* 令人驚奇的；不可思議的；很棒的
cute〔kjut〕*adj.* 可愛的　　ugly〔'ʌglɪ〕*adj.* 醜陋的
strange〔strendʒ〕*adj.* 奇怪的　　pet〔pɛt〕*v.* 撫摸
feed〔fid〕*v.* 餵食　　enjoy〔ɪn'dʒɔɪ〕*v.* 喜歡
perform〔pɚ'fɔrm〕*v.* 表演

Museums are cool, *too*.	博物館也很棒。
The exhibits are terrific.	那些展覽品很棒。
The displays are fascinating.	那些展示品很吸引人。
I like famous things.	我喜歡有名的作品。
I enjoy works of art.	我喜歡藝術品。
Maybe someday my work	也許有一天，我的作品會
will be there.	放在那裡。
History tells me about the past.	歷史告訴我過去的事。
Science shows me the future.	科學告訴我未來的情況。
From dinosaurs to robots, I	從恐龍到機器人，我全部
love it all.	都愛。

＊＊ —————————————————

museum〔mju'ziəm〕*n.* 博物館；美術館
cool〔kul〕*adj.* 很棒的　　exhibit〔ɪg'zɪbɪt〕*n.* 展覽品
terrific〔tə'rɪfɪk〕*adj.* 很棒的　　display〔dɪ'sple〕*n.* 展示品
fascinating〔'fæsn̩,etɪŋ〕*adj.* 吸引人的；迷人的
famous〔'feməs〕*adj.* 有名的　　thing〔θɪŋ〕*n.* 作品；事物
work〔wɝk〕*n.* 作品　　art〔ɑrt〕*n.* 藝術
maybe〔'mebɪ〕*adv.* 也許
someday〔'sʌm,de〕*adv.* (將來) 有一天
history〔'hɪstrɪ〕*n.* 歷史　　past〔pæst〕*n.* 過去
science〔'saɪəns〕*n.* 科學　　show〔ʃo〕*v.* 告訴；告知
future〔'fjutʃɚ〕*n.* 未來　　dinosaur〔'daɪnə,sɔr〕*n.* 恐龍
robot〔'robət〕*n.* 機器人　　love〔lʌv〕*v.* 愛

8

Finally, *amusement parks are a blast*.	最後我要說的是，遊樂園是最好玩的。
I'm crazy about wild rides.	我很喜歡瘋狂的遊樂設施。
Roller coasters are the best.	雲霄飛車是最棒的。
It's fun to scream.	尖叫很有趣。
It's fun to be scared.	被嚇到很好玩。
I don't care if I get dizzy.	我不在乎自己會不會頭暈。
Hey, I'm curious about you.	嘿，我對你們很好奇。
Where do you like to go?	你們喜歡去哪裡？
What's your favorite place?	你們最喜歡的地方是哪裡？

8

** ─────────────────

finally〔'faɪnḷɪ〕*adv.* 最後　　amusement〔ə'mjuzmənt〕*n.* 娛樂
amusement park 遊樂園　　blast〔blæst〕*n.* 歡樂；滿足
crazy〔'krezɪ〕*adj.* 很喜歡的 <*about*>
wild〔waɪld〕*adj.* 瘋狂的
ride〔raɪd〕*n.* (娛樂場所的) 乘坐物；遊樂設施
roller coaster 雲霄飛車　　best〔bɛst〕*n.* 最好的事物
fun〔fʌn〕*adj.* 有趣的　　scream〔skrim〕*v.* 尖叫
scared〔skɛrd〕*adj.* 受驚嚇的　　care〔kɛr〕*v.* 在乎
dizzy〔'dɪzɪ〕*adj.* 頭暈的　　hey〔he〕*interj.* 嘿
curious〔'kjʊrɪəs〕*adj.* 好奇的

背景說明

　　你最喜歡去什麼地方呢？有很多小朋友喜歡去麥當勞，喜歡去遊樂場或主題樂園玩。本篇演講稿要教你介紹自己喜歡去的那些地方，無論你喜歡去什麼地方，都可以套用這篇演講稿來告訴大家。

1. ***Here are three of my favorites***.

favorite〔ˈfevərɪt〕*n.* 最喜歡的人、事、物

　　favorite 主要是當形容詞，作「最喜歡的」解，在這裡當名詞用，作「最喜歡的地方」解。這句話的意思是「以下是我最喜歡的三個地方。」也可以說成：These three are my favorites. (這是我最喜歡的三個地方。)

　　Here is/are~ 的句型，美國人常說，例如：

Here's your coffee. (你的咖啡來了。)
Here are some glasses. (這裡有一些玻璃杯。)
Here is a little gift I bought for you.
(這是我買給你的小禮物。)

coffee〔ˈkɔfɪ〕*n.* 咖啡
glass〔glæs〕*n.* 玻璃杯　　　gift〔gɪft〕*n.* 禮物

【比較】 在 Here is/are 的句型中，若主詞為代名詞，則要放在 is/are 的前面，例如：

Here you are. (你要的東西在這裡；拿去吧。)【正】
Here are you.【誤】

8

2. ***The animals are amazing.***

animal〔ˈænəml̩〕*n.* 動物
amazing〔əˈmezɪŋ〕*adj.* 令人驚奇的；不可思議的；很棒的

　　　　amazing 的主要意思是「令人驚奇的」，凡是看到好的東西或好的事情，即使不那麼驚奇，美國人也喜歡用這個字來誇張，相當於 incredible（不可思議的）或 really great（很棒的）。

　　　　The animals are amazing. 字面的意思是「那些動物令人驚奇。」引申為「那些動物眞是不可思議。」或「那些動物很棒。」

美國人常用 amazing 來稱讚好的事物，如：

　　The show was ***amazing***.（這個表演眞是太棒了。）
　　The meal she cooked was ***amazing***.
　　（她煮的飯眞是太棒了。）
　　Our school trip was ***amazing***.
　　（我們學校的旅行太棒了。）

　　　　amazing 也可以用在名詞前面，強調某事物很棒，例如：She has an ***amazing*** talent for music.（她在音樂方面有驚人的才能。）【talent〔ˈtælənt〕*n.* 才能】

3. ***Some are cute and some are ugly.***

cute〔kjut〕*adj.* 可愛的　　ugly〔ˈʌglɪ〕*adj.* 醜的

　　　　這句話的意思是：「牠們有些很可愛，有些很醜。」比如説，大家都覺得企鵝和無尾熊很可愛，但是像蛇和蜥蜴，可能就會有人覺得牠們很醜。

4. ***I like to pet and feed them***.

pet〔pɛt〕*v.* 撫摸

feed〔fid〕*v.* 餵食

　　這句話的意思是「我喜歡摸牠們，還有餵牠們吃東西。」

　　這句話還可以說成：

I enjoy touching them and giving them food.

（我喜歡摸牠們，還有給牠們食物。）

It's fun to touch them and give them
　　something to eat.

（摸牠們還有給牠們東西吃很有趣。）

【touch〔tʌtʃ〕*v.* 觸摸　　food〔fud〕*n.* 食物】

　　pet 在這裡是作「撫摸」解，是當動詞用，但是這個字也很常當名詞用，作「寵物」解，例如：

No ***pets*** allowed.（請勿攜帶寵物入內。）

Dogs and cats are the most popular ***pets***.

（狗和貓是最受歡迎的寵物。）

allow〔ə'lau〕*v.* 允許…進入

most〔most〕*adv.* 最

popular〔'pɑpjələ〕*adj.* 受歡迎的

注意：pet（撫摸）不要和 pat〔pæt〕*v.* 輕拍搞混。

　　　如：I always ***pat*** my dog when I get home.

　　　　（我回到家時，總是會拍拍小狗的頭。）

8

5. ***I enjoy works of art.***

   work〔wɝk〕*n.* 作品　　art〔ɑrt〕*n.* 藝術

　　work 主要是當動詞用，作「工作」解，例如：
My dad ***works*** very hard.（我爸很努力工作。）但
在這裡 work 是名詞，當「作品」解。所以這句話的
意思是「我喜歡藝術品。」也可以説成：

   I really like artwork.（我很喜歡藝術品。）
   I like all kinds of art.（我喜歡各種藝術品。）

   really〔'rɪəlɪ〕*adv.* 非常；眞地
   artwork〔'ɑrt,wɝk〕*n.* 藝術品
   art〔ɑrt〕*n.* 藝術品

下面都是 work 當「作品」解的例子：

   She likes Shakespeare's ***works***.
   （她喜歡莎士比亞的作品。）
   Van Gogh painted over 800 ***works*** of art
   　in just two years.
   （梵谷兩年內就畫了超過八百幅藝術作品。）
   Museums in Paris have the most famous
   　works of art.
   （巴黎的美術館擁有最著名的藝術品。）

   paint〔pent〕*v.* 畫　　over〔'ovɚ〕*prep.* 超過
   museum〔mju'zɪəm〕*n.* 博物館；美術館
   famous〔'feməs〕*adj.* 有名的

6. *Finally*, *amusement parks are a blast*.

finally〔'faınlı〕*adv.* 最後

amusement〔ə'mjuzmənt〕*n.* 娛樂

amusement park 遊樂園　　blast〔blæst〕*n.* 歡樂；滿足

　　這句話的意思是「最後我要說的是，遊樂園是最好玩的。」blast 字面的意思是「歡樂；滿足」，引申為「非常好玩的事物；非常快樂的時光」(= *lots of fun* ; *wonderful time*)。所以，這句話也可以說成：

Amusement parks are lots of fun.
（遊樂園很好玩。）

Amusement parks are exciting.
（遊樂園很刺激。）

【fun〔fʌn〕*n.* 樂趣　　exciting〔ɪk'saɪtɪŋ〕*adj.* 刺激的】

blast 這個字的用法，舉例說明如下：

Our school graduation trip was a *blast*!
（我們學校的畢業旅行很好玩！）

I had a *blast* on New Year's Eve with my cousins.
（除夕夜那晚，我和我的表兄弟姊妹玩得很開心。）

We had a *blast* playing video games last weekend.（上個週末，我們打電動打得很開心。）

graduation〔,grædʒʊ'eʃən〕*n.* 畢業

trip〔trɪp〕*n.* 旅行　　*New Year's Eve* 除夕

cousin〔'kʌzn̩〕*n.* 表（堂）兄弟姊妹

video games 電動玩具　　weekend〔'wik'ɛnd〕*n.* 週末

8

7. **I'm crazy about wild rides**.

crazy〔'krezɪ〕adj. 狂熱的；很喜歡的（和 about 連用）
wild〔waɪld〕adj. 瘋狂的
ride〔raɪd〕n. （娛樂場所的）乘坐物；遊樂設施

　　這句話的意思是「我很喜歡瘋狂的遊樂設施。」
ride 通常是當動詞用，作「騎；乘」解，但在這裡
是當名詞用，作「（娛樂場所的）乘坐物；遊樂設施」
解，像是旋轉木馬或雲霄飛車，都可以用這個字。

這句話也可以說成：

I really enjoy the fast and scary rides.
（我很喜歡快速而嚇人的遊樂設施。）

I just love the exciting rides.
（我就是愛那些刺激的遊樂設施。）

fast〔fæst〕adj. 快的
scary〔'skɛrɪ〕adj. 嚇人的
just〔dʒʌst〕adv. 正好；恰好
exciting〔ɪk'saɪtɪŋ〕adj. 刺激的

be crazy about 就是「很喜歡；為…瘋狂」的意
思，以下都是美國人常講的話：

He **is crazy about** kung fu movies.
（他很喜歡功夫片。）

Jennifer **is crazy about** shopping.
（珍妮佛很喜歡購物。）
【shopping〔'ʃɑpɪŋ〕n. 購物】

8

My Favorite Places

Many people have favorite places they like to go to when they are feeling sad or bored. I, too, have favorite places that I go to as often as I can.

Here are the three places that I like most. *First of all*, I like the zoo. The animals are amazing because some are so cute and some are so ugly! I like to pet them, feed them and watch them perform. Museums are cool places, too. They have good exhibits and fascinating displays. I like the works of art there. Some museums teach me a lot about history and science. From dinosaurs to robots, I love it all. *Finally*, theme parks are a blast. I love to go on the wild rides. I think the roller coasters are the best. It's fun to scream and get scared.

These places always cheer me up. I try to go to each of my favorite places once a year. I am going to find more favorite places to go to when I grow up.

8

● 中文翻譯

我最喜歡的地方

　　許多人都有最喜歡的地方，當他們覺得難過或無聊時，就喜歡去那些地方。我也有喜歡的地方，而且我會儘量常去這些地方。

　　以下是我最喜歡的三個地方。首先，我喜歡動物園。動物真是不可思議，因為牠們有些很可愛，有些很醜！我喜歡摸牠們，餵牠們吃東西，還有看牠們表演。博物館也很棒。它們有很棒的展覽品，和很吸引人的展示品。我喜歡那裡的藝術品。有些博物館會教我很多與歷史和科學有關的知識。從恐龍到機器人，我全部都愛。最後，主題樂園是最好玩的。我喜歡乘坐瘋狂的遊樂設施。我覺得雲霄飛車是最棒的。尖叫和受到驚嚇都很有趣。

　　這些地方總是會讓我開心。我每年都會試著去一次每個我最喜歡的地方。等我長大以後，我還要去發掘更多最喜歡的地方。

8

9. My Motto

I have a super motto.
It works like magic.
It's "just do your best."

I say it all the time.
It guides me every day.
It's helpful in many ways.

It helps me face challenges.
It takes away my worries.
It makes me feel stronger, too.

9

motto ('mɑto)	super ('supɚ)
work (wɝk)	magic ('mædʒɪk)
just (dʒʌst)	best (bɛst)
do one's best	*all the time*
guide (gaɪd)	helpful ('hɛlpfəl)
way (we)	face (fes)
challenge ('tʃælɪndʒ)	*take away*
worry ('wɝɪ)	strong (strɔŋ)

One day I was sick.

I had an important test.

I was very nervous and afraid.

I told myself, "Just do your best.

Give your best effort.

Give one hundred percent."

Then I had courage.

I became confident.

As a result, I did a wonderful job.

one day	sick〔sɪk〕
important〔ɪmˈpɔrtṇt〕	test〔tɛst〕
nervous〔ˈnɝvəs〕	afraid〔əˈfred〕
myself〔maɪˈsɛlf〕	effort〔ˈɛfɚt〕
hundred〔ˈhʌndrəd〕	percent〔pɚˈsɛnt〕
then〔ðɛn〕	courage〔ˈkɝɪdʒ〕
become〔bɪˈkʌm〕	
confident〔ˈkɑnfədənt〕	
result〔rɪˈzʌlt〕	***as a result***
wonderful〔ˈwʌndɚfəl〕	job〔dʒɑb〕

9

Please follow this motto.
Say it every day.
You can benefit, too.

Don't worry about the outcome.
Don't compare yourself with others.
Just do your best.

I believe anything is possible.
Where there's a will, there's a way.
So please do your best every day.

follow ('fɑlo)   benefit ('bɛnəfɪt)
outcome ('aʊt͵kʌm)
compare (kəm'pɛr)   believe (bɪ'liv)
anything ('ɛnɪ͵θɪŋ)   possible ('pɑsəbl̩)
will (wɪl)   way (we)

9

9. My Motto

演講解說

I have a super motto.	我有一個很棒的座右銘。
It works like magic.	它就像魔法一樣有效。
It's "just do your best."	它就是「只要盡力就好」。
I say it all the time.	我總是會說這句話。
It guides me every day.	它引導我過每一天。
It's helpful in many ways.	它在很多方面都有幫助。
It helps me face challenges.	它幫助我面對挑戰。
It takes away my worries.	它消除我的憂慮。
It makes me feel stronger, too.	它還使我覺得更堅強。

9

** ─────

motto〔'mɑto〕*n.* 座右銘　　super〔'supə〕*adj.* 極好的

work〔wɜk〕*v.* 有效；起作用　　magic〔'mædʒɪk〕*n.* 魔法

just〔dʒʌst〕*adv.* 只要　　best〔bɛst〕*n.* 最大的努力　*adj.* 最好的

do one's best 盡力　　*all the time* 經常；總是

guide〔gaɪd〕*v.* 引導　　helpful〔'hɛlpfəl〕*adj.* 有幫助的

way〔we〕*n.* 方面　　face〔fes〕*v.* 面對

challenge〔'tʃælɪndʒ〕*n.* 挑戰　　*take away* 消除

worry〔'wɜɪ〕*n.* 憂慮　*v.* 擔心　　strong〔strɔŋ〕*adj.* 堅強的

One day I was sick.

I had an important test.

I was very nervous and afraid.

I told myself, "Just do your
   best.

Give your best effort.

Give one hundred percent."

Then I had courage.

I became confident.

As a result, I did a wonderful
   job.

有一天，我生病了。

我有一場很重要的考試。

我非常緊張和害怕。

我告訴自己：「只要盡力
就好。

盡你最大的努力。

百分之百地付出。」

然後我有了勇氣。

我變得有自信。

結果，我考得很好。

＊＊ ──────────────

one day 有一天　　sick〔sɪk〕*adj.* 生病的

important〔ɪm'pɔrtn̩t〕*adj.* 重要的　　test〔tɛst〕*n.* 考試

nervous〔'nɜvəs〕*adj.* 緊張的　　afraid〔ə'fred〕*adj.* 害怕的

myself〔maɪ'sɛlf〕*pron.* 我自己　　effort〔'ɛfɚt〕*n.* 努力

hundred〔'hʌndrəd〕*adj.* 一百的

percent〔pɚ'sɛnt〕*n.* 百分之…　　then〔ðɛn〕*adv.* 然後

courage〔'kɜɪdʒ〕*n.* 勇氣　　become〔bɪ'kʌm〕*v.* 變得

confident〔'kɑnfədənt〕*adj.* 有自信的

result〔rɪ'zʌlt〕*n.* 結果　　**as a result** 結果

wonderful〔'wʌndɚfəl〕*adj.* 極好的　　job〔dʒɑb〕*n.* 事物

9

Please follow this motto.	請遵循這個座右銘。
Say it every day.	每天都說這句話。
You can benefit, too.	你也會從中獲益。
Don't worry about the outcome.	不要擔心結果。
Don't compare yourself with others.	不要拿別人和自己比較。
Just do your best.	只要盡力就好。
I believe anything is possible.	我相信任何事都有可能。
Where there's a will, there's a way.	有志者，事竟成。
So please do your best every day.	所以請你們每天都要盡力。

9

** ───────────────

follow〔ˈfɑlo〕v. 遵循　benefit〔ˈbɛnəfɪt〕v. 獲益
outcome〔ˈaʊtˌkʌm〕n. 結果　compare〔kəmˈpɛr〕v. 比較
believe〔bɪˈliv〕v. 相信　anything〔ˈɛnɪˌθɪŋ〕pron. 任何事
possible〔ˈpɑsəbḷ〕adj. 可能的　will〔wɪl〕n. 意志力
way〔we〕n. 路；方法
Where there's a will, there's a way. 【諺】有志者，事竟成。

● **背景說明**

　　「座右銘」就是古代讀書人，放在座位右邊的書桌上，用來砥礪自己的一句話。「銘」本來是「刻在木頭上或石頭上」，表示「很重要的話」。本篇演講稿，要教你用英文來介紹自己的座右銘，把影響你最深的一句話，告訴週遭的人，幫助他們從中獲益。

1. *It works like magic.*

　　work〔wɜk〕*v.* 有效；起作用　　magic〔'mædʒɪk〕*n.* 魔法

　　　　work 的主要意思是「工作」，可當名詞或動詞用，但在這裡，是作「有效；起作用」解，例如：

　　Compliments can *work* well in cheering
　　　others up.（讚美可以有效地使人振作。）

　　The medicine *worked* so quickly, I was
　　　surprised.（這種藥的藥效快到令我驚訝。）

　　compliment〔'kɑmpləmənt〕*n.* 稱讚
　　cheer up 使振作；使高興　　medicine〔'mɛdəsn̩〕*n.* 藥物
　　surprised〔sə'praɪzd〕*adj.* 驚訝的

　　　　這句話的意思是「它就像魔法一樣有效。」也可說成：

　　It works so well that it's hard to believe.
　　（它是如此有效，令人難以置信。）

　　It's so good; it's miraculous.
　　（它很棒；它很不可思議。）

　　【miraculous〔mə'rækjələs〕*adj.* 不可思議的】

9

2. *Just do your best.*

just〔dʒʌst〕*adv.* 只要　　best〔bɛst〕*n.* 最大的努力
do one's best 盡力

　　這句話的意思是「只要做到你最大的努力。」也就
是「只要盡力就好。」以下都是美國人常說的話,我們
按照使用頻率排列:

① *Just do your best.*(只要盡力就好。)【第一常用】
② Try your hardest.(要非常努力。)【第二常用】
③ Do the best you can do.【第三常用】
　　(盡你所能去做。)

④ Give it your all.(要全力以赴。)

⑤ Give your very best effort.
　　(要付出你最大的努力。)
　　very〔'vɛrɪ〕*adv.* 真正地;全然
　　best〔bɛst〕*adj.* 最好的;最大的

　　另外,美國人很喜歡在動詞前面加 just,來加強
動詞,作「只是」解,例如:

Just wait here; I'll be right back.
(就在這裡等;我馬上回來)

Just apologize and I'll forgive you.
(只要道歉,那麼我就會原諒你。)

wait〔wet〕*v.* 等待　　right〔raɪt〕*adv.* 馬上;立即
back〔bæk〕*adv.* 回原處
apologize〔ə'pɑlə,dʒaɪz〕*v.* 道歉
forgive〔fɚ'gɪv〕*v.* 原諒

9

3. *It helps me face challenges*.

face〔fes〕*v.* 面對　　challenge〔'tʃælɪndʒ〕*n.* 挑戰

　　　face 的基本意思是「臉」，是當名詞用，但在這裡是當動詞用，作「面對」(= *confront*) 解。所以這句話的意思是「它幫助我面對挑戰。」也可以說成：

It assists me in doing difficult tasks. (它幫助我做困難的工作。)

【assist〔ə'sɪst〕*v.* 幫助　　task〔tæsk〕*n.* 工作】

4. *It takes away my worries*.

take away 帶走；消除　　worry〔'wɝɪ〕*n.* 憂慮

　　　這句話的意思是「它消除我的憂慮。」也可以說成：

It gets rid of my fears. (它消除我的憂慮。)

It makes my troubles go away.
(它使我的煩惱消失。)

get rid of 消除　　fear〔fɪr〕*n.* 憂慮；恐懼
trouble〔'trʌbḷ〕*n.* 煩惱　　*go away* 消失

9

　　　另外，*take away* 這個片語有三個比較常見的用法：

① 作「消除」解。例如：

I'll give you some pills to *take away*
the pain. (我會給你一些藥丸來止痛。)

【pill〔pɪl〕*n.* 藥丸　　pain〔pen〕*n.* 痛】

② 作「減掉」(= *deduct*) 解。例如：

Take away 2 from 5 and you get 3.
（5 減 2 等於 3。）

③ 作「拿走」解。例如：

My parents *took* my comic books *away*.
（我爸媽把我的漫畫書拿走。）

parents〔'pɛrənts〕*n. pl.* 父母
comic〔'kɑmɪk〕*adj.* 漫畫的

5. *Give your best effort.*
Give one hundred percent.

give〔gɪv〕*v.* 給；付出
best〔bɛst〕*adj.* 最大的
effort〔'ɛfət〕*n.* 努力
hundred〔'hʌndrəd〕*adj.* 一百的
percent〔pə'sɛnt〕*n.* 百分之…

這兩句話的意思是「盡你最大的努力。百分之百地付出。」其實這兩句話，意義相同，目的是要加強語氣。美國人還有很多類似的說法，我們依照使用頻率排列如下：

① *Give your best effort.*【第一常用】
② *Give one hundred percent.*【第二常用】
③ Do your very best.【第三常用】
（你要盡力而為。）
【very〔'vɛrɪ〕*adv.* 真正地；全然】

9

④ Try as hard as you can. (盡你所能地努力。)

⑤ Go all out. (盡全力。)

⑥ Give it all you've got. (付出你的所有。)

hard〔hɑrd〕*adv.* 努力地　　***try hard*** 盡力而為

as…as** one can* 儘可能　　***go all out 盡全力

have got 擁有

6. *As a result, I did a wonderful job.*

result〔rɪˈzʌlt〕*n.* 結果　　***as a result*** 結果；因此

wonderful〔ˈwʌndəˌfəl〕*adj.* 極好的

job〔dʒɑb〕*n.* 工作；事物

　　這句話字面的意思是「結果，我做了很棒的事。」引申為「結果，我考得很好。」也可以說成：Consequently, I really did well. (結果，我真的考得很好。)

consequently〔ˈkɑnsəˌkwɛntlɪ〕*adv.* 因此；結果

do well 考得好

　　美國人喜歡說 ***do a ~job***，意思是「做得~；表現得~」，例如：

The lazy student *did an* awful *job* on the test.

(這名懶惰的學生在這次的考試中，表現得很糟。)

I always try to *do a* good *job*.

(我總是努力把事情做好。)

The team *did an* excellent *job* at the sports

　　meet. (這支隊伍在運動大會中，表現得非常好。)

lazy〔ˈlezɪ〕*adj.* 懶惰的　　awful〔ˈɔful〕*adj.* 很糟的

team〔tim〕*n.* 隊　　excellent〔ˈɛksḷənt〕*adj.* 極好的

sports〔sports〕*adj.* 運動的　　meet〔mit〕*n.* 大會

9

7. ***Where there's a will, there's a way.***

will 〔 we 〕 *n.* 意志力   way 〔 we 〕 *n.* 路；方法

　　這句話是美國發明家愛迪生
（ Thomas Edison ）說的，意思
就是「有志者，事竟成。」愛迪生
在發明燈泡之前，總共失敗了兩
千多次，但是在他眼中，那些失敗的經驗，都是幫助
他找出正確方法的必經之路。學英文也是一樣，我們
已經幫你找到正確的方法 —— 背「一口氣兒童英語演
講」，所以只要你持之以恆地把每一篇演講稿背下來，
不用多久，你的英文就可以說得比美國人好。

這句話還可以說成：

If you try hard enough, you'll succeed.
（ 如果你夠努力，你就會成功。）

Great determination will lead to success.
（ 堅定的決心會使你成功。）

Never give up and you'll get what you want.
（ 永不放棄，那麼你就會得到你想要的。）

Always keep trying and you'll always
　achieve!
（ 一直不斷嘗試，那麼你一定會做到！）

enough 〔 ə'nʌf 〕 *adv.* 足夠地
succeed 〔 sək'sid 〕 *v.* 成功   great 〔 gret 〕 *adj.* 大的
determination 〔 dɪ,tɜmə'neʃən 〕 *n.* 決心
lead to 導致   success 〔 sək'sɛs 〕 *n.* 成功
give up 放棄   achieve 〔 ə'tʃiv 〕 *v.* 達到；達成

○作文範例

My Motto

Do you know what mottos are? They are things people say that have a special meaning. I have a super motto and it works like magic. My motto is "Just do your best."

I say it all the time. My motto guides me every day. It's very helpful to me. It helps me face challenges and takes away my worries. It makes me feel stronger, too. *For example*, I was sick on a day that I had an important test. I was very nervous and afraid, so I told myself, "Just do your best." *Then*, I tried my best. I gave it one hundred percent and I did a great job.

This motto can make you confident. Don't worry about what will happen and don't compare yourself to other people. Just do your best, and you will be fine. Anything is possible if you do your best, so try to do your best every day.

9

● 作文範例

我的座右銘

　　你知道什麼是座右銘嗎？座右銘就是人們說的，具有特別意義的話。我有一個很棒的座右銘，而且它跟魔法一樣有效。我的座右銘就是「只要盡力就好」。

　　我總是會說這句話。我的座右銘引導我過每一天。它對我很有幫助。它幫助我面對挑戰，並消除我的憂慮。它還使我覺得更堅強。舉例來說，有一天，我生病了，而且我有個重要的考試。我非常緊張和害怕，所以我告訴我自己：「只要盡力就好。」然後，我試著盡力，並百分之百地付出，結果我考得很好。

　　這個座右銘可以使你有信心。不要擔心會發生什麼事，也不要拿自己和別人比較。只要盡力，你就會做得很好。如果你盡力，那麼任何事都有可能，所以每天都要試著盡力。

9

10. My Future Plan

I'm excited about my future.
I have big hopes and dreams.
Here's what I want to do.

I'll study hard.
I'll get excellent grades.
I'll be the best I can be.

I want to study overseas.
I want to learn a lot.
My dream school is Harvard University.

future〔'fjutʃɚ〕   plan〔plæn〕
excited〔ɪk'saɪtɪd〕   hope〔hop〕
dream〔drim〕   hard〔hɑrd〕
excellent〔'ɛksl̩ənt〕   grade〔gred〕
best〔bɛst〕   overseas〔͵ovɚ'siz〕
Harvard〔'hɑrvɚd〕   university〔͵junə'vɝsətɪ〕

10

I might be a teacher.

I might be a doctor.

I might be a scientist.

I want to help people out.

I want to be useful to society.

No matter what, I'll be an expert at

what I do.

I want to be rich, too.

I want to make a lot of money.

I want to make my family proud.

---

might〔maɪt〕

doctor〔'dɑktɚ〕

help sb. out

society〔sə'saɪətɪ〕

expert〔'ɛkspɝt〕

make〔mek〕

proud〔praʊd〕

teacher〔'titʃɚ〕

scientist〔'saɪəntɪst〕

useful〔'jusfəl〕

no matter what

rich〔rɪtʃ〕

a lot of

10

I'd like to travel.

I want to see the world.

I want to visit every country.

I hope to meet many people.

I hope to make many friends.

I want to experience different
   cultures.

Now I wish you good luck.

Have a wonderful future.

May all your dreams come true.

I'd like to	travel ('trævl̩)
world (wɜld)	visit ('vɪzɪt)
country ('kʌntrɪ)	meet (mit)
make friends	experience (ɪk'spɪrɪəns)
different ('dɪfərənt)	culture ('kʌltʃɚ)
wish (wɪʃ)	luck (lʌk)
wonderful ('wʌndɚfəl)	may (me)
true (tru)	*come true*

10

10. My Future Plan

演講解說

I'm excited about my future.	我對自己的未來感到很興奮。
I have big hopes and dreams.	我有遠大的希望和夢想。
Here's what I want to do.	以下就是我想要做的事。
I'll study hard.	我會用功唸書。
I'll get excellent grades.	我會拿到很好的成績。
I'll be the best I can be.	我會盡我所能成爲一個佼佼者。
I want to study overseas.	我想要出國唸書。
I want to learn a lot.	我想要學很多東西。
My dream school is Harvard University.	哈佛大學是我理想的學校。

10

**

future〔ˈfjutʃɚ〕*adj.* 未來的　*n.* 未來　　plan〔plæn〕*n.* 計劃

excited〔ɪkˈsaɪtɪd〕*adj.* 感到興奮的　　hope〔hop〕*n.,v.* 希望

dream〔drim〕*n.* 夢想　*adj.* 理想的

hard〔hɑrd〕*adv.* 努力地　　　excellent〔ˈɛksḷənt〕*adj.* 優秀的

grade〔gred〕*n.* 成績　　best〔bɛst〕*adj.* 最好的

the best 佼佼者　　overseas〔ˌovɚˈsiz〕*adv.* 在國外

Harvard〔ˈhɑrvɚd〕*n.* 哈佛　　university〔ˌjunəˈvɝsətɪ〕*n.* 大學

I might be a teacher.	我可能會當老師。
I might be a doctor.	我可能會當醫生。
I might be a scientist.	我可能會當科學家。
I want to help people out.	我想要幫助人們。
I want to be useful to society.	我想成為對社會有用的人。
No matter what, I'll be an expert at what I do.	無論如何，我都會成為我那一行的專家。
I want to be rich, too.	我還想要有錢。
I want to make a lot of money.	我想要賺很多錢。
I want to make my family proud.	我想要讓我的家人以我為榮。

** ———————————————————

might〔maɪt〕*aux.* 可能會　　teacher〔'titʃə〕*n.* 老師
doctor〔'dɑktə〕*n.* 醫生　　scientist〔'saɪəntɪst〕*n.* 科學家
help sb. out 幫助某人（ = *help sb.*）
useful〔'jusfəl〕*adj.* 有用的
society〔sə'saɪətɪ〕*n.* 社會　　*no matter what* 無論如何
expert〔'ɛkspɜt〕*n.* 專家　　rich〔rɪtʃ〕*adj.* 有錢的
make〔mek〕*v.* 賺（錢）；使
proud〔praʊd〕*adj.* 驕傲的；感到光榮的

10

I'd like to travel.	我想要去旅行。
I want to see the world.	我想要看看世界。
I want to visit every country.	我想要到每一個國家去遊覽。
I hope to meet many people.	我希望認識很多人。
I hope to make many friends.	我希望結交很多朋友。
I want to experience different cultures.	我想要體驗不同的文化。
Now I wish you good luck.	現在，我要祝你們好運。
Have a wonderful future.	祝你們有美好的未來。
May all your dreams come true.	但願你們的夢想全都成眞。

** ——————————————————

I'd like to 我想要 (= *I would like to* = *I want to*)

travel〔'trævḷ〕*v.* 旅行　　visit〔'vɪzɪt〕*v.* 參觀；遊覽

country〔'kʌntrɪ〕*n.* 國家　　meet〔mit〕*v.* 認識

make friends 交朋友　　experience〔ɪk'spɪrɪəns〕*v.* 體驗

different〔'dɪfərənt〕*adj.* 不同的

culture〔'kʌltʃə〕*n.* 文化　　wish〔wɪʃ〕*v.* 祝

luck〔lʌk〕*n.* 運氣　　wonderful〔'wʌndəfəl〕*adj.* 美好的

may〔me〕*aux.* 但願　　true〔tru〕*adj.* 眞的

come true 成眞；實現

10

背景說明

　　你將來長大之後，想要做什麼呢？你的夢想是什麼呢？夢想通常會隨著時間而不斷改變，小時候想當總統，長大以後，可能卻當了醫生。本篇演講稿，要教你介紹自己的夢想，把你未來的計劃和大家分享。

1. *Here's what I want to do.*

　　這句話的意思是「以下就是我想要做的事。」

　　what 一般是作疑問代名詞，例如：What's your name?（你叫什麼名字？）但在這裡，what 是兼做先行詞的複合關係代名詞，代替 the thing which，所以這句話是從 Here's the thing which I want to do. 轉化而來的。也可說成：Let me tell you my plan.（讓我告訴你我的計劃。）

【plan〔plæn〕*n.* 計劃】

　　what 當複合關係代名詞的用法，舉例如下：

Please tell me *what* you did last night.
（請告訴我你昨晚做了什麼事。）
Let me tell you *what* to do.
（讓我來告訴你要做什麼事。）【*last night* 昨晚】

10

2. ***I'll be the best I can be.***

best〔bæst〕*adj.* 最好的　　***the best*** 佼佼者

　　　　這句話是由 I'll be the best person I can be.
省略而來的，the best 在這裡是指 the best student
或 the best person。所以整句
話的意思是「我會盡我所能成
爲一個佼佼者。」也可說成：

　　　I'll go as far as I can go.
　　　（我會盡力。）

　　　I'll try hard to achieve my potential.
　　　（我會努力發揮自己的潛能。）

　　　go as far as *one* ***can go***　盡力
　　　hard〔hɑrd〕*adv.* 努力地　　achieve〔ə'tʃiv〕*v.* 達到
　　　potential〔pə'tɛnʃəl〕*n.* 潛能

3. ***My dream school is Harvard University.***

dream〔drim〕*adj.* 理想的　　Harvard〔'hɑrvəd〕*n.* 哈佛
university〔ˌjunə'vɝsətɪ〕*n.* 大學

　　　　這句話的意思是「哈佛大學是我理想的學校。」
也可以說成：

　　　Going to Harvard University would be a dream
　　　　come true.（去唸哈佛大學就是美夢成眞。）

　　　I hope and pray I can go to Harvard University.
　　　（我希望並祈禱能去唸哈佛大學。）

　　　【***come true*** 成眞；實現　　pray〔pre〕*v.* 祈禱】

　　另外，dream 一般是作「夢想」解，可當名詞或動詞用，例如：Dreams sometimes come true.（夢想有時會成真。）但在這裡，dream 是當形容詞用，作「理想的」解，例如：

A house on the beach would be my *dream* home.（海邊的房子是我理想的家。）

My *dream* vacation would be a trip to Europe.（我理想中的假期是到歐洲去旅行。）

My *dream* weekend would be going to Disneyland.（我理想中的週末是到狄斯奈樂園去。）

Being an English teacher would be my *dream* job.（當英文老師是我的理想工作。）

house〔haʊs〕*n.* 房子　　beach〔bitʃ〕*n.* 海灘
vacation〔veˈkeʃən〕*n.* 假期　　trip〔trɪp〕*n.* 旅行
Europe〔ˈjʊrəp〕*n.* 歐洲　　weekend〔ˈwikˈɛnd〕*n.* 週末
Disneyland〔ˈdɪznɪˌlænd〕*n.* 狄斯奈樂園
job〔dʒɑb〕*n.* 工作

10

　　每個人都有夢想，而俗話說得好：「工欲善其事，必先利其器。」不管你未來的夢想是什麼，在這個國際化的時代，你一定要先把英文學好，那麼你的夢想才能早日實現。

4. ***No matter what*, *I'll be an expert at what I do*.**

no matter what 無論如何　　expert〔'ɛkspɝt〕*n.* 專家

　　　這句話的意思是「無論如何,我都會成為我那一行的專家。」what 在這裡一樣是兼做先行詞的複合關係代名詞,代替 the job which。這句話也可以說成：Whatever happens, I'll be great at my job.

（無論發生什麼事,我都會專精於我的工作。）

whatever〔hwɑt'ɛvɚ〕*pron.* 無論何事
happen〔'hæpən〕*v.* 發生　　job〔dʒɑb〕*n.* 工作

　　　no matter what 是作「無論如何」解 (= *in any case*)。

　　　下面是美國人常說的話：

***No matter what*, never lie, cheat or steal.**
（無論如何,絕對不要說謊、騙人,或偷東西。）

Always listen to your parents ***no matter what*.**
（無論如何,一定要聽你爸媽的話。）

***No matter what*, I'll always love my country.**
（無論如何,我一定會愛國。）

never〔'nɛvɚ〕*adv.* 絕不　　lie〔laɪ〕*v.* 說謊
cheat〔tʃit〕*v.* 欺騙　　steal〔stil〕*v.* 偷竊
always〔'ɔlwez〕*adv.* 總是;一定
listen〔'lɪsn̩〕*v.* 聽　　parents〔'pærənts〕*n. pl.* 父母
love〔lʌv〕*v.* 愛　　country〔'kʌntrɪ〕*n.* 國家

10

5. ***I want to make my family proud***.

make〔mek〕*v.* 使　　proud〔praʊd〕*adj.* 光榮的

這句話是從：I want to make my family proud of me. 省略而來的，意思是「我想要讓我的家人以我為榮。」也可以說成：I want my parents to be proud of me. （我想要讓我的父母以我為榮。）

另外，make + sb. + adj. 就是「使某人感到…的」的意思，例如：

Wisdom ***makes*** you strong.
（知識使你堅強。）

The surprise gift ***made*** him very happy.
（這個意外的禮物使他非常開心。）

Her behavior ***made*** her family very ashamed.
（她的行為使她的家人感到非常羞愧。）

The rainy weather ***made*** everyone gloomy.
（多雨的天氣使得每個人悶悶不樂。）

wisdom〔'wɪzdəm〕*n.* 智慧；知識
strong〔strɔŋ〕*adj.* 堅強的
surprise〔sə'praɪz〕*adj.* 使人感到意外的
gift〔gɪft〕*n.* 禮物　　behavior〔bɪ'hevjɚ〕*n.* 行為
ashamed〔ə'ʃemd〕*adj.* 感到羞愧的
rainy〔'renɪ〕*adj.* 多雨的　　weather〔'wɛðɚ〕*n.* 天氣
gloomy〔'glumɪ〕*adj.* 悶悶不樂的

10

6. ***Now I wish you good luck*.**

wish〔wɪʃ〕*v.* 祈願；祝　　luck〔lʌk〕*n.* 運氣

　　這句話的意思是「現在，我要
祝你們好運。」當你要祝福別人時，
就可以用 wish 這個字，你有兩種
說法可以選擇：

　　① 「wish ＋ 人 ＋ 名詞」，例如：

　　　　I ***wish*** you a Merry Christmas.

　　　　（我祝你聖誕快樂。）

　　② 「wish ＋ 名詞 ＋ to ＋ 人」，例如：

　　　　He ***wished*** success to all his students.

　　　　（他祝福他所有的學生成功。）

　　　　merry〔'mɛrɪ〕*adj.* 快樂的
　　　　Christmas〔'krɪsməs〕*n.* 聖誕節
　　　　success〔sək'sɛs〕*n.* 成功

7. ***May all your dreams come true*.**

may〔me〕*aux.* 但願　　　dream〔drim〕*n.* 夢想
true〔tru〕*adj.* 眞的　　***come true*** 成眞；實現

　　這句話的意思是「但願你們的夢想全都成眞。」
may 這個字也可以用來祝福別人，「May ＋ 主詞
＋ 原形動詞」是祈願句，如：

　　May you live to be one hundred.

　　　（祝你活到一百歲。）【hundred〔'hʌndrəd〕*n.* 百】

　　May you always have good health.

　　　（祝你永遠健康。）【health〔hɛlθ〕*n.* 健康】

作文範例

My Future Plan

Everybody dreams about the future. There are many things waiting for us in the future, and sometimes I can't wait to become an adult. I'm excited about my future because I have big hopes and dreams.

Here's what I want to do. I plan to study hard because I want to go to a school overseas. My dream school is Harvard University. I might be a teacher, a doctor or a scientist. No matter what, I'll be an expert at what I do so I can be useful to society. I want to be rich, too. I want to make a lot of money so my family will be proud of me. I also like to travel, so I want to visit every country and see the world. I hope to meet many people and make many friends.

I am determined to make my dreams come true. I know it won't be easy, but when I do make my dreams come true, I'll be the happiest person in the world.

10

● 中文翻譯

我未來的計劃

　　每個人對於未來都有夢想。未來有很多事等著我們去做，所以有時候我會等不及要變成大人。我對於自己的未來感到很興奮，因為我有遠大的希望與夢想。

　　以下就是我想要做的事。我打算努力唸書，因為我想要出國唸書。我理想的學校就是哈佛大學。我可能會當老師、醫生，或科學家。無論如何，我會成為我那一行的專家，這樣我才能當一個對社會有用的人。我還想要有錢。我想要賺很多錢，這樣我的家人就會以我為榮。我也喜歡旅遊。所以我要去每個國家遊覽，並看看這個世界。我希望認識很多人，然後交很多朋友。

　　我下定決心要實現我的夢想。我知道那並不容易，但是當我真的實現夢想時，我會是全世界最快樂的人。

這10篇演講稿，
你都背下來了嗎？
現在請利用下面的提示，
不斷地複習。

以下你可以看到每篇演講稿的格式，三句為一組，九句為一段，每篇演講稿共三段，27句，看起來是不是輕鬆好背呢？不要猶豫，趕快開始背了！每篇演講稿只要能背到50秒之內，就終生不忘！

1. Self-introduction

Ladies and gentlemen:
I'm happy to be here.
I'd like to introduce myself.

My name is Pat.
Everyone calls me Pat.
You can call me Pat.

I'm from Taiwan.
I was born in Taiwan.
I grew up in Taiwan.

Right now, I'm a student.
I'm eager to learn.
I study very hard every day.

I like being a student.
I like going to school.
I think it's interesting and fun.

I'm also learning English.
I enjoy speaking English.
It's my favorite class.

I'm a friendly person.
I always try to be polite.
I like to get along with everyone.

I want to be your friend.
I hope we can meet.
What do you say?

Let's be friends.
Let's get together.
Please introduce yourself.

2. My Hobbies

I have many hobbies.
I like to do many things.
Let me share a few.

I like video games.
Computer games are cool, too.
I could play them all day.

I like collecting cards.
I play games with them.
I trade them with my friends.

Also, I like sports.
I like being outdoors.
I love fresh air and sunshine.

Bike riding is fun.
Rollerblading is neat.
Swimming is my favorite.

In addition, I like to draw pictures.
I like to read comics.
But please don't tell my parents.

Furthermore, I like music.
I like to sing songs.
I'm learning to play an instrument.

Of course, I enjoy learning English.
I like speaking with foreigners.
I love watching Disney cartoons.

There is more I like to do.
There is more I can say.
I'll save it for another day.

3. My Family

I have a wonderful family.
I'm lucky to be a part of it.
Let me tell you about them.

My family name is Lee.
My family history is long and ….
There are five people in my ….

My parents love me very much.
They do a lot for me.
When I need help, they are ….

My dad is a strong guy.
He's honest and hardworking.
He's like a superhero to me.

My mom is a smart woman.
She can do almost anything.
I just can't praise her enough.

I have two siblings.
They are my older brother and ….
Sometimes we argue, but we ….

My family likes being together.
We like eating out and going to ….
We also enjoy hiking and having ….

My family isn't perfect.
We have our ups and downs.
But we always forgive and make up.

Our motto is "United together ….
I'll always cherish my family.
I hope your family is lovely, too.

4. My Best Friend

I have a best friend.
We met at school.
We're in the same grade.

He's a diligent student.
He's very hardworking.
I learn a lot from him.

He helps me with math.
I help him with English.
We're a good study team.

He's honest and reliable.
I trust him completely.
We share secrets all the time.

He's loyal and brave.
Once a bully teased me.
He came to my rescue right away.

He's considerate and polite.
He makes me little gifts.
He always remembers my birthday.

He is fun to be with.
He tells funny jokes.
His stories make me laugh.

He's a good listener.
He knows when I'm blue.
He picks me up when I'm down.

He's one of a kind.
We'll stay friends forever.
I hope you have a friend like mine.

5. My Daily Schedule

My day is typical.
I bet it's like yours.
Let me tell you my routine.

My alarm goes off at 6:30.
I take my time getting up.
I rise and shine with a stretch.

I take off my PJ's.
I wash up quickly.
I brush my teeth and comb my hair.

I put on my uniform.
I pack my backpack for school.
Then, I put on my sneakers and ….

I never skip breakfast.
I eat at home or on the way.
But I always eat in a hurry.

After school, I go to a cram school.
I hit the books again there.
I finish my homework for the day.

Finally, I return home.
I relax and take a break.
I have dinner with my family.

I watch some TV.
I go to bed around 9:30.
I fall asleep right away.

On weekends, everything is ….
I sleep late and have a ball.
Is your day the same as mine?

6. My School Life

I love school.
I think school is really cool.
Let me tell you about my school ….

I go to school five days a week.
I'm there eight hours each day.
School is a big part of my life.

My school day is long.
My schedule is so full.
There is always something going ….

My teachers are excellent.
They help me to improve.
They are very patient and kind.

My classmates are good friends.
We often study together.
We always help each other out.

We are like a team.
We play games and enjoy activities.
We laugh and have fun when we ….

My schoolwork keeps me busy.
I have homework every day.
I have quizzes and tests all the time.

I like learning new things.
I know knowledge is power.
I'm preparing for the future.

My school is like a family.
It's like a home away from home.
I hope you feel the same way ….

7. My Favorite Teacher

I have a favorite teacher.
Her name is Miss Lee.
She is so wonderful to me.

She has a sweet personality.
She's very patient and kind.
She never gets angry or yells.

She encourages me.
She compliments my efforts.
She makes me feel special all the ….

Her class is interesting.
We do many different things.
We never feel tired or bored.

She's charming and bright.
She's an expert for sure.
She answers every question we ask.

She demands a lot.
She gives lots of homework.
But we always work hard to ….

The little things make her great.
Her smile warms my heart.
Her simple praise is music to my ….

She's a good listener.
She's very understanding.
She's fair to everyone.

She brightens up my day.
I'll never forget her.
I'll remember her forever.

8. My Favorite Place

I like many places.
I enjoy many spots.
Here are three of my favorites.

I'll start with the zoo.
The animals are amazing.
Some are cute and some are ugly.

Some are very strange.
I like to pet and feed them.
I enjoy seeing them perform.

Museums are cool, too.
The exhibits are terrific.
The displays are fascinating.

I like famous things.
I enjoy works of art.
Maybe someday my work will ….

History tells me about the past.
Science shows me the future.
From dinosaurs to robots, I love ….

Finally, amusement parks are a ….
I'm crazy about wild rides.
Roller coasters are the best.

It's fun to scream.
It's fun to be scared.
I don't care if I get dizzy

Hey, I'm curious about you.
Where do you like to go?
What's your favorite place?

9. My Motto

I have a super motto.
It works like magic.
It's "just do your best."

I say it all the time.
It guides me every day.
It's helpful in many ways.

It helps me face challenges.
It takes away my worries.
It makes me feel stronger, too.

One day I was sick.
I had an important test.
I was very nervous and afraid.

I told myself, "Just do your best.
Give your best effort.
Give one hundred percent."

Then I had courage.
I became confident.
As a result, I did a wonderful job.

Please follow this motto.
Say it every day.
You can benefit, too.

Don't worry about the outcome.
Don't compare yourself with others.
Just do your best.

I believe anything is possible.
Where there's a will, there's a way.
So please do your best every day.

10. My Future Plan

I'm excited about my future.
I have big hopes and dreams.
Here's what I want to do.

I'll study hard.
I'll get excellent grades.
I'll be the best I can be.

I want to study overseas.
I want to learn a lot.
My dream school is Harvard ….

I might be a teacher.
I might be a doctor.
I might be a scientist.

I want to help people out.
I want to be useful to society.
No matter what, I'll be an expert ….

I want to be rich, too.
I want to make a lot of money.
I want to make my family proud.

I'd like to travel.
I want to see the world.
I want to visit every country.

I hope to meet many people.
I hope to make many friends.
I want to experience different ….

Now I wish you good luck.
Have a wonderful future.
May all your dreams come true.

新一代英語教科書・領先全世界

學習語言以口說為主・是全世界的趨勢

本書所有人

姓名 ＿＿＿＿＿＿＿＿＿＿＿＿ 電話 ＿＿＿＿＿＿＿＿＿＿＿

地址 ＿＿＿＿＿＿＿＿＿＿＿＿＿＿＿＿＿＿＿＿＿＿＿＿＿＿

（如拾獲本書，請通知本人領取，感激不盡。）

「一口氣兒童英語演講①」背誦記錄表

篇　　　　　　　　　　名	口試通過日期	口試老師簽名
1. Self-introduction	年　　月　　日	
2. My Hobbies	年　　月　　日	
3. My Family	年　　月　　日	
4. My Best Friend	年　　月　　日	
5. My Daily Schedule	年　　月　　日	
6. My School Life	年　　月　　日	
7. My Favorite Teacher	年　　月　　日	
8. My Favorite Places	年　　月　　日	
9. My Motto	年　　月　　日	
10. My Future Plan	年　　月　　日	
全部 10 篇演講總複試	年　　月　　日	

　　自己背演講，很難專心，背給別人聽，是最有效的方法。練習的程序是：自己背 ➡ 背給同學聽 ➡ 背給老師聽 ➡ 在全班面前發表演講。可在教室裡、任何表演舞台或台階上，二、三個同學一組練習，比賽看誰背得好，效果甚佳。

　　天天聽著 CD，模仿美國人的發音和語調，英文自然就越說越溜。英語演講背多後，隨時都可以滔滔不絕，口若懸河。